Attack of the Video Villains

After a few minutes, Joe's taxicab left the city and began meandering across open countryside.

"Uh-oh," said Chet. "Now things are going to get tough. It's the Attack of the Killer Sports Cars!"

Frank sat on the edge of his seat as a half dozen sleek black automobiles materialized and zeroed in on Joe's taxi.

"What are you going to do now, Joe?" Frank asked.

"Use the oil slick!" Chet urged.

Sure enough, a rainbow-hued pool of liquid appeared directly behind Joe's cab. One of the black cars plowed into it at full speed and began spinning wildly until it hit a bridge abutment and disappeared in a flash of colored particles.

"Whoops, here comes another one," Chet said.

"Oh, no!" Frank cried. "A head-on collision! Joe, you'd better do something fast!"

The Hardy Boys Mystery Stories ®

#59   Night of the Werewolf
#60   Mystery of the Samurai Sword
#61   The Pentagon Spy
#62   The Apeman's Secret
#63   The Mummy Case
#64   Mystery of Smugglers Cove
#65   The Stone Idol
#66   The Vanishing Thieves
#67   The Outlaw's Silver
#68   Deadly Chase
#69   The Four-headed Dragon
#70   The Infinity Clue
#71   Track of the Zombie
#72   The Voodoo Plot
#73   The Billion Dollar Ransom
#74   Tic-Tac-Terror
#75   Trapped at Sea
#76   Game Plan for Disaster
#77   The Crimson Flame
#78   Cave-in!
#79   Sky Sabotage
#80   The Roaring River Mystery
#81   The Demon's Den
#82   The Blackwing Puzzle
#83   The Swamp Monster
#84   Revenge of the Desert Phantom
#85   The Skyfire Puzzle
#86   The Mystery of the Silver Star
#87   Program for Destruction
#88   Tricky Business
#89   The Sky Blue Frame
#90   Danger on the Diamond
#91   Shield of Fear
#92   The Shadow Killers
#93   The Serpent's Tooth Mystery
#94   Breakdown in Axeblade
#95   Danger on the Air
#96   Wipeout
#97   Cast of Criminals
#98   Spark of Suspicion
#99   Dungeon of Doom
#100 The Secret of the Island Treasure
#101 The Money Hunt
#102 Terminal Shock
#103 The Million-Dollar Nightmare
#104 Tricks of the Trade
#105 The Smoke Screen Mystery
#106 Attack of the Video Villains

Available from MINSTREL Books

106

The HARDY BOYS®

ATTACK OF THE VIDEO VILLAINS

FRANKLIN W. DIXON

A MINSTREL® BOOK

PUBLISHED BY POCKET BOOKS

New York   London   Toronto   Sydney   Tokyo   Singapore

This book is a work of fiction. Names, characters, places and incidents are either the product of the author's imagination or are used fictitiously. Any resemblance to actual events or locales or persons, living or dead, is entirely coincidental.

A MINSTREL PAPERBACK *ORIGINAL*

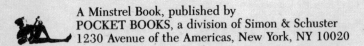

A Minstrel Book, published by
POCKET BOOKS, a division of Simon & Schuster
1230 Avenue of the Americas, New York, NY 10020

Copyright © 1991 by Simon & Schuster Inc.
Cover artwork copyright © 1991 by Paul Bachem
Produced by Mega-Books of New York, Inc.

ISBN: 0-671-67275-5

First Minstrel Books printing February 1991

10 9 8 7 6 5 4 3 2 1

THE HARDY BOYS MYSTERY STORIES is a trademark of Simon & Schuster

THE HARDY BOYS, A MINSTREL BOOK and colophon are registered trademarks of Simon & Schuster

Printed in U.S.A.

Contents

1.   *Hack Attack*   1
2.   *Video Game Heaven*   14
3.   *Back Doors*   27
4.   *The Men from Omega*   38
5.   *The Japanese Connection*   49
6.   *Let the Games Begin!*   59
7.   *The Final Four*   68
8.   *Industrial Espionage*   76
9.   *The Mystery Solved?*   84
10. *Smoke Screen*   96
11. *Interrupted Tournament*   106
12. *The Secret of Hack Attack*   113
13. *The Real Cartridge Thief*   121
14. *Into the Underground*   132
15. *Quick Escape*   143

ATTACK OF THE
VIDEO VILLAINS

1 Hack Attack

"Look out for that truck, Joe!" Frank Hardy cried over the sound of the roaring engine.

Joe Hardy looked up to see a green garbage truck cut directly across his path. With lightning-fast reflexes, he steered his compact taxicab out of the way of the truck and onto the sidewalk, coming within inches of hitting the truck's front bumper. Two terrified pedestrians, who had the misfortune to be on the sidewalk just as Joe made his unexpected detour, leapt out of the way in the nick of time.

"Wow!" shouted Chet Morton admiringly from his seat just behind Joe's right shoulder. "Incredible driving!"

"Yeah," agreed Frank, who was seated next to

Chet. "That's your last cab. And if you'd hit those pedestrians, you'd have lost your bonus round. Nice going."

"Thanks, guys," said Joe, glancing briefly at his companions. "Now, keep it down, will you? I can't concentrate on this game with you guys carrying on."

Joe turned back to the television screen in front of him, his blue eyes alert. His muscular six-foot frame looked as if it was ready for action as he played the game. Although there was a family resemblance between Joe and his brother, Joe's blond hair contrasted with Frank's dark hair. Brown-eyed Frank stood an inch taller than his brother and, at eighteen, was a year older. Their husky friend Chet had curly brown hair and a jovial smile.

The image they were all watching on the screen was a network of winding city streets viewed from high above, as though the player were looking down at the city from somewhere in the clouds. A tiny red taxicab raced through the streets while multicolored cars and antlike pedestrians darted in and out of its path. With a small plastic game controller gripped in his hand, Joe nimbly guided the taxi through this urban maze.

In a corner of the spacious hotel room, the three boys were seated in comfortable armchairs pulled up around the television on which Joe was

2

playing his video game. Atop a wooden table next to the TV sat a black plastic video game console, connected to the television by a series of wires. A bright blue game cartridge poked out of the top of the console.

"No question about it," said Chet to Frank. "Your brother's one of the best Hack Attack players in the world. *Número uno!*"

"You don't have to tell *me* that," said Frank. "That's why we're here in New York City, remember? I don't know about you, but I came here to see Joe officially acknowledged as the number one video game player in the United States."

"I'm only in it for the money," said Joe with mock modesty. On the screen, his taxicab came squealing to a halt at a red traffic light. "Fifty thousand dollars. That'll sure buy a lot of video game cartridges."

"Yeah, sure," Frank chided. "You love this game and you know it. Ever since you got that cartridge, I can't even get you to come outside and play football. You'd be playing it right now even if you *weren't* a finalist in the National Hack Attack Tournament."

"Well, maybe," said Joe with a laugh. "I guess this game's gotten into my blood. Now be quiet. I want to finish this round."

"Uh-oh," said Chet. "Looks like you're surrounded."

Joe frowned at the screen. The cab was in the

3

middle of an intersection, and vehicles were coming at it from all sides. A fire engine squealed its way down one street while a police car flew from the opposite direction. A lumbering bus and a large truck came from the other two directions.

"Whoops," said Joe. "I'm trapped."

"Use the laser beam," suggested Chet.

"I'm out of laser beams," said Joe. "There's nothing I can do. I guess this is the end of the game."

Suddenly, the sound of celestial music poured out of the television. A pair of flickering orange wings appeared in front of Joe's cab.

"I don't believe it!" Joe cried. "The magic wings! I'm saved!"

"All right!" Chet exclaimed. "Get those wings and leave those other guys behind!"

Joe revved the taxi forward and ran over the wings, which promptly vanished. The taxicab glowed bright orange for a moment, then sprouted a pair of airplanelike wings on both sides. With a roar, it took off and soared over the tops of the other vehicles, which collided in a vividly colored explosion.

"Head for Detroit!" suggested Frank. "You can buy another cab there at the factory."

"No," said Chet. "Head for Dallas. You can hook up to an oil well and fill up your fuel tank."

"Nope," said Joe. "I'm going to Atlanta to drop off my passenger, remember? If I don't get him to his destination, I don't get the fare—and I don't gain any points. Then I'm going back to New York. That's where you can pick up the most passengers. And if I don't pick up passengers . . ."

"I get the drift," said Chet.

As the taxi soared upward, the streets and buildings seemed to drop away and were replaced by fleecy white clouds. The taxi soared through the sky as Joe guided it with the controller. Occasional glimpses of the ground appeared through holes in the clouds.

"This is *my* favorite part of the game," said Joe, leaning back in his chair and relaxing. "Nothing to do but steer the cab and watch the clouds roll by."

"Yeah, sure." Frank laughed. "You'll be bored silly in twenty seconds. I bet your favorite part is where you have to cross the Mississippi River on a ferry and dodge the submarines."

"Nah," said Chet. "I bet your favorite part is where you get beamed up by the starship and get chased by the alien cybertanks."

"None of the above," said Joe, leaning back and spreading his arms expansively. "My *real* favorite part is where—"

"Hey!" exclaimed Chet. "What's that?"

"What's what?" asked Joe, hunching forward toward the screen.

Directly in front of the flying taxicab, a large

5

eaglelike bird was soaring lazily through the clouds. It was twice as big as the cab and was moving so slowly that there was no way it was going to get out of the path of the cab in time.

"Oh, no!" shouted Joe. "The bird!"

He frantically tried to move the controller, but the cab responded too slowly. It struck the bird at full speed, sending a burst of feathers scattering in all directions. The bird scowled at the cab and flew away angrily. The cab plunged back toward the ground, its wings broken and crumpled.

"I don't believe it!" moaned Joe. "I hit the bird! I should have been watching where I was going!"

"I guess this is definitely *not* your favorite part of the game anymore," said Frank, as Joe slumped back into his chair. Joe watched miserably as the cab struck the ground in a bright orange explosion. Then the image faded to black and the words "GAME OVER" appeared in large white letters on the screen.

"Better not do that in the tournament," advised Chet.

"Thanks," said Joe sullenly. "At least I won't have you guys to distract me."

"That's right," said Chet. "Blame it on us!"

"Hey, guys," said Frank, standing up and stretching his limbs. "I'm tired of sitting around this hotel room. Let's go down to the lobby and see if we can meet some of the other contestants."

"Sounds good," said Joe, dropping the video game controller onto a table and switching off the game console. "I think I've had enough Hack Attack practice for one day."

The three teenagers filed out of the hotel room and into the elegant hallway, where the plush red carpets made a sharp contrast with their blue jeans and T-shirts. Frank locked the door, then led the way to the mirror-lined elevator.

"Nice place," said Chet, as they entered the elevator. "Maybe we can try the room service when we get back."

"Let me guess," said Joe. "You'll have them send up a meal for three, then you'll lock the two of us in the bathroom and eat it all yourself."

"Hey, that's a great idea," said Chet with a grin. "Why didn't I think of that?"

"It was only a matter of time," said Joe.

When the elevator opened in the hotel lobby, Joe smiled in anticipation as he read a banner draped along the ceiling: The Videomundo Corporation Welcomes the Hack Attack Champions! Scattered between the words were humorous caricatures of a taxicab, with headlights shaped like eyes and a smiling mouth for a grille.

"Hack Attack champion!" said Chet. "That's you, Joe!"

7

"And a couple of dozen other people," Joe responded. "I won't be the champion until the tournament is over, the day after tomorrow."

"We have the utmost faith in you," said Frank. "You *are* going to split that fifty thousand with your brother, aren't you?"

"Not on your life," said Joe.

"Excuse me," said a teenager standing underneath the banner. "Are you here for the tournament?"

"Joe is," said Chet. "Frank and I just came to watch him."

"Hi, Joe!" said the young man, extending his hand for a shake. "My name's Jason Tanaka. Nick Phillips and I"—he gestured to the teenager standing next to him—"came down to meet some of the other contestants. We're both finalists, too."

"Hey, nice to meet you, Jason," said Joe, returning the shake. "You, too, Nick. This is my brother, Frank Hardy, and my friend Chet Morton."

Joe stood back and appraised the newcomers. Jason was slender and handsome, about five feet nine inches tall in his sneakers, and had straight black hair. He was dressed in a yellow knit shirt and black denim pants. Nick was heavyset, with red hair and a round face. He wore a casual pair of shorts and a black T-shirt with the name of a popular rock band on it.

8

"We were just on our way to a swap meet," Jason said. "Want to join us?"

"Swap meet?" asked Frank.

"Yeah," said Nick, holding up a paper bag filled with video game cartridges. "A bunch of the contestants are getting together and swapping Videomundo cartridges. If you brought some along, you can trade them for new games."

"As a matter of fact, I did," said Joe. "How about you guys?" Joe asked Frank and Chet.

"I've got a few tucked away in my luggage," answered Chet. "This sounds great. Let's go back up to the room and get them."

"I'm afraid I didn't bring any," said Frank. "Mind if I tag along?"

"No problem," said Jason.

Agreeing to meet Jason and Nick at the swap meet fifteen minutes later, Frank, Joe, and Chet returned to their room for the cartridges. When they got back downstairs, the swap meet was already under way in a small, crowded room off the main lobby. Joe stood at the doorway, watching a throng of video game players happily passing cartridges back and forth, arguing the relative merits of various games. Jason was standing next to one wall negotiating a transaction with a young man dressed in baggy shorts and a loose shirt. Jason looked toward the door and motioned for Joe and his friends to join him.

"There's some great stuff here," Jason

announced, waving a plastic cartridge. "I just got a copy of Battle of the Barbarians. I've been wanting to play this for months."

"And I found the Adventures of Bobbity Babbit Three," added Nick, who stood a few feet away holding up another cartridge. "I loved the first two games, and this one is supposed to be even better."

"Wow!" Chet exclaimed. "I love the Bobbity Babbit games! Anybody got any more?"

"I do," said someone in the far corner of the room. Chet eagerly shoved his way through the crowd.

A half hour later, Joe and Chet emerged from the room with broad smiles on their faces, each carrying a bag full of video games in their hands. Frank trailed after them, looking a little puzzled about all the excitement.

"I still don't see how you can get so excited over a game about a purple rabbit who gets superpowers every time he eats a carrot," Frank said to Chet.

"I'm telling you, Frank, this Bobbity Babbit game is great," said Chet. "When you eat a green carrot, you can kill the bad guys by just breathing on them!"

"I've known some guys like that," said Joe. "So what games did you get besides Bobbity Babbit?"

"Take a look," said Chet, holding his bag out

10

where Joe could see it. "There's some great stuff in here."

Joe reached into the bag and began rummaging around. "You've got a copy of Hack Attack in here. Why not just play mine?"

Chet looked a little sheepish. "I wanted my own copy. I figure if I play it enough, maybe I can be in the tournament next year."

"Great idea!" said Joe, slapping Chet on the back and dropping the Hack Attack cartridge into the bag. "We'll start a Bayport dynasty! I'll win the tournament this year, then you can win it next year!"

"Of course, you'll have to live up to the standards set by Joltin' Joe Hardy," added Frank.

"Wait up, guys!" cried a voice from the room where the swap meet was still in progress. Joe turned to see Jason Tanaka coming toward them.

"Hey, Jason," said Joe, looking at the bulging bag in the teenager's hand. "Looks like you found a few good games, too."

"I got all sorts of great stuff!" he agreed. "I'll have to show it to you later."

"What happened to Nick?" asked Frank. "Is he still in there?"

"No, he left already," Jason said. "He'll catch up with us later."

"So what do you guys want to do?" Joe asked. "The opening ceremonies aren't for a couple of hours yet."

"Let's go eat," suggested Chet.

"I'm not even hungry," said Joe. "We only had lunch two hours ago."

"Well, I'm hungry," said Chet. "I vote that we go for dinner now."

"You're *always* hungry," said Frank.

"Do you want to come along, Jason?" asked Joe.

"Sure! There's a little diner on the corner," said Jason. "We could stop and have sodas while Chet has something to eat."

"Sounds great," said Chet. "Let's go!"

"Wait a minute," said Jason, nodding toward the other end of the lobby. "There's Bill Longworth. He must not have been at the swap meet."

"Bill who?" asked Frank, turning in the direction of Jason's nod. Coming across the plush carpet, he saw a tall young man of about twenty in a blazer, with carefully slicked-back brown hair and a self-assured, almost arrogant expression on his face.

"Oh, yeah," said Joe. "Last year's tournament champion. I'd like to meet him."

Joe walked toward the tall man and extended his hand. "Hello, Bill. I'm Joe Hardy. I've been hoping for a chance to meet you."

Longworth looked Joe over from head to toe. "You're *who?* One of the contestants, I suppose."

"That's right," said Joe. "I saw the videotapes

12

of your winning game last year. You were really great."

"Of course I was," said Longworth. "I'm the best Hack Attack player in the world. Now, if you'll excuse me, I have an appointment to meet someone." Without so much as a second glance, he strode across the lobby and out the front door.

"Well, there goes Mr. Personality," said Frank, after Longworth had departed. "I don't suppose success has gone to that guy's head."

"He should definitely have his head examined," said Joe. "What a jerk!"

"I should have warned you," said Jason. "Bill Longworth has a reputation for being, well, difficult to get along with."

"Difficult isn't the word for it," said Joe.

"I'd like to remind you that we were about to go eat," said Chet.

"Oh, right," said Joe. "Let's get—"

Joe's sentence was interrupted by the sound of running footsteps. A small man with dark hair and a faded denim jacket bolted across the room, heading straight toward Joe. The younger Hardy braced himself for a collision, but instead of plowing into Joe, the figure turned suddenly and snatched the bag of video game cartridges from Joe's hand.

Then he turned and raced for the front door, the bag clutched tightly in his hands, and disappeared into the street!

2 Video Game Heaven

Joe stood stunned, gaping after the departed thief. "I don't believe it! That guy stole my video games!"

"Let's get him!" shouted Chet, racing toward the door.

"Right!" cried Joe, running after Chet. Frank followed right behind them.

Frank ran outside and paused at the top of the steps that led to the main entrance of the hotel. He looked past the taxicabs that lined the curb waiting for fares and spotted the scruffy thief sprinting past the last cab.

"This way!" Frank shouted, pointing to the left.

"He's fast!" yelled Joe. "I wish I'd worn my running shoes!"

"Speed is the first job requirement for purse snatchers and video game thieves," replied Frank, propelling himself past the last cab and into the street.

The driver of a large car hit his brakes and skidded to a halt a few feet from Frank. "Watch where you're goin'!" the driver yelled at the top of his lungs. "You wanna put a dent in my fender?"

"Sorry," muttered Frank. The thief was already at the next street corner, rapidly disappearing from sight.

"Don't let him get away," yelled Chet. But by the time they had rounded the corner, the thief was nowhere to be seen.

"Terrific!" said Joe. "He got away. And with my bag full of games!"

"We'll call the cops," said Frank. "Maybe they can get the games back."

"Oh, sure," said Joe. "Ten video game cartridges somewhere in the biggest city in the Western Hemisphere. I'm sure they'll have them back by breakfast."

"Well, it's worth a try," Frank said as he, Joe, and Chet turned back toward the hotel.

"Speaking of breakfast . . ." Chet began.

15

"Yeah, yeah," said Joe. "We were going out for a snack. First we'd better report this."

When they entered the lobby, Frank spotted Jason Tanaka standing next to an older man in an expensive suit. He had sandy blond hair cut stylishly long and a concerned look on his face.

"Joe," said Jason. "Did you get your games back?" When Joe shook his head, Jason added, "This is Steve Lewis. He's the representative from Videomundo who's managing the tournament. I've already told him what happened."

"I want to apologize for this incident," said Lewis in grave tones. "If you'll come down to my office, we'll contact the police and hotel security. And the Videomundo Corporation will be glad to replace the games that you lost. We're very concerned about this breach of security. Very concerned."

"Oh," said Joe. "Well, thanks. Sure, I'll come down to your office. You guys want to come along?"

"Fine with me," said Frank.

Steve Lewis's office was a makeshift facility in a corridor off the main lobby of the hotel. Frank looked around as he entered and saw that the room was small and cramped. It contained a desk stacked with papers, several telephones, and a coffee machine surrounded by unwashed cups. Joe sat on a metal folding chair while Steve made

16

the necessary phone calls. Chet, Frank, and Jason stood by the coffee machine and waited.

Two security men arrived a few moments later and questioned the teenagers about the theft. The security guards promised to tell the police to be on the lookout for a thief matching the description they had been given.

"I'm afraid I'm going to have to rush off now," said Steve Lewis when the guards left. "It's almost time for the opening ceremonies, and I'm a scheduled speaker. Get back to me later, Joe, and I'll see about replacing those cartridges."

"Thanks," said Joe. "We'll see you at the ceremonies."

Once they were back out in the hallway, Frank turned to the others. "Well, I guess it's off to the ceremonies, right?"

"What about my snack?" asked Chet.

"Too late, Chet," said Joe. "You'll have to keep your appetite under control for at least another hour."

"So where are these ceremonies being held?" asked Frank.

"Next door at the convention center," said Joe.

"Right," said Jason. "That's why they chose this hotel for the contestants. There's a door down here at the end of the hallway that goes directly into the convention center."

"Lead on," said Joe. "I want to get a front row seat."

17

As they entered the convention center, Joe resisted the urge to gape. The building was so new it sparkled, and it was about ten times larger than Joe had expected. The hallway where they entered was decorated with chrome trim and plush carpets. Joe wondered if the hall might not go on forever. The foyer at the main entrance was more spacious than some entire buildings that Joe had been in. Modern chandeliers hung from the ceiling, and crowds of people milled about on the gold carpet. Large television screens were mounted on the walls, with computerized advertisements and schedules flashing on them.

"What a place," said Joe. "This makes the Bayport Convention Center look tiny."

"This makes the Bayport Convention Center look like the local Moose Lodge," said Frank.

"Looks like we're on time," said Jason, pointing at one of the televised schedules. It read: 3:00 PM—Videomundo Tournament Opening Ceremonies.

"We've got fifteen minutes to spare," said Frank. "Let's find a seat."

The room where the tournament was to be held looked to Frank like the interior of a sports coliseum. A large sunken floor was surrounded on all sides by tiers and tiers of seats. A special seating section had been set aside for the Hack Attack players and their guests. Joe grabbed a block of seats as close to the front as he could get, and he, Frank, Chet, and Jason settled into their seats. A few minutes later, Nick appeared. He had changed into a pair of long pants and a blue blazer.

"Hey, Nick!" said Jason, gesturing him to an open seat. "Welcome back. You're just in time."

"Sorry I missed all the excitement," Nick said. "I hear you guys had a little run-in with the seedier side of New York."

"Where'd you hear that?" Joe inquired.

"Word travels fast around here," said Nick, settling into his seat. "Everybody's heard about the theft. I even heard that there have been a couple more."

"What?" exclaimed Frank. "More thefts? Like the one that happened to Joe?"

"Yeah," said Nick. "Apparently only about ten minutes after Joe got hit on, two more contestants who had been to the swap meet had their game cartridges swiped a block away from the hotel."

"If you were going to steal video games," said Frank, "I can think of worse places you could hang out. Practically everybody around here seems to be carrying some games with them."

Chet glanced down at his own bag of video games, which he held clutched tightly in his lap. "I'm not letting anybody get hold of these. I'm protecting them with my life!"

"Sure," said Joe. "You'd trade those games for a good corned beef sandwich in no time."

19

Chet raised one eyebrow. "Think somebody'd make the offer?"

"Maybe I'd better hang on to those games," said Frank. "I don't want Chet's stomach making him do something he'll later regret."

"Hey, I was just kidding," said Chet. "I'd insist on at least *two* corned beef sandwiches. And they'd definitely have to be on rye."

A high-pitched whine came from a stage on the floor below, where somebody was adjusting a microphone.

"Looks like things are about to get under way," said Jason. "There's Steve Lewis." He pointed toward the stage, where the Videomundo representative was chatting with several other men in dark suits.

"Those guys must all be from Videomundo," said Frank. "I guess they consider this a very important occasion."

"Of course," said Jason. "This whole contest is a big-time promotion for the Videomundo Corporation. After all, the Hack Attack game is published by Videomundo. And it can only be played on the Videomundo Game Console, which we gamers like to call the VGC. A lot of newspapers and TV stations are covering the tournament, so Videomundo should get a lot of publicity out of this."

Joe pointed at a number of men and women in similarly dark suits seated not far from the contestants' section. "Are those guys from Videomundo, too?"

"I don't think so," said Jason. "I recognize a couple of them. I've seen their pictures in video game magazines. They're from Omega, Videomundo's chief rival."

"Oh, yeah," said Chet. "They make the Omega Super System. I hear it's not as good as the Videomundo."

"It's all right," said Jason, "but most of the best games are from Videomundo."

"You sure know a lot about video games," said Frank to Jason.

"You'd better believe it," said Nick. "He's been filling my ear all morning with all kinds of information about these games. And I thought that *I* was an expert . . . until I met Jason, anyway."

"I guess it's in my blood," said Jason. "My parents are from Japan, and this whole video game craze got its start there, you know."

"I'd heard that," said Frank. "I'd like to know more about it."

"We can talk about it later," said Jason. "As far as I'm concerned, the only thing more fun than talking about video games is actually playing them."

"It looks like Steve Lewis is about to speak," said Nick. "Better listen up."

Steve Lewis bent over the microphone and

cleared his throat. The sound boomed out of the huge overhead speakers like rumbling thunder.

"I'd like to welcome all of you to the Second Annual National Hack Attack Tournament," he began, "sponsored by the Videomundo Corporation of America. My name is Steve Lewis, and I'll be your host for the weekend. On behalf of the Videomundo Corporation, I'd like to thank both the contestants and the audience for their interest in our games."

There was a mild scattering of applause from the audience in the arena. Steve smiled and nodded his head in acknowledgment.

"As many of you know, the Videomundo Corporation has had an extremely successful three years in America, ever since the introduction of the Videomundo Game Console here. We know that many families now enjoy following the adventures of the popular Videomundo character Bobbity Babbit—or, of course, playing a lively round of Hack Attack!"

The mention of the name Hack Attack drew a spirited cheer from quite a few members of the audience, particularly in the area where the contestants were seated. Joe joined in, letting out a loud whistle and clapping at the reference to his favorite game.

Steve Lewis smiled. "Hack Attack has been on the market for two years now, and it's still a best-seller. But Hack Attack isn't the only game

22

you can play on your Videomundo Game Console. In fact, I'd like to show you some scenes from half a dozen *new* games that will be released over the next three months."

High overhead, six large television screens suspended from the ceiling came to life. Joe looked up to see the image of a colorful, fast-moving video game appear on each screen. Bizarre alien creatures and tiny men and women ran and jumped across obstacle courses, and spaceships zapped everything in their path with energy beams.

"This is awesome," said Chet.

"This is incredible!" Jason exclaimed. "I've got to get every one of these games!"

"Me, too," said Nick. "I can't stand the thought that there's a video game out there somewhere that I don't own."

"You've all gone nuts," said Frank. "I mean, video games are fun and all, but don't you want to get into anything else?"

"Spoilsport," said Joe, giving his brother a dirty look. "Those games do look pretty neat. I guess I'll be saving up my pennies, too."

"I thought you were going to win fifty thousand dollars," Frank reminded him.

"Oh, right," said Joe.

When the presentation of the new games was over, Steve Lewis read off the names of the two-dozen contestants in the Hack Attack Tournament. Each stood and took a bow, as the audience clapped politely. When it was Joe's turn, he waved enthusiastically at the spectators, like an athlete taking his turn on the field.

"Why didn't you hold up a sign that said, Hi, Mom!" Frank joked.

"I didn't think of that," said Joe with a smile. "Mom'll probably be watching, too. This is supposed to be on the six o'clock news back in Bayport."

To wrap up his presentation, Steve Lewis mentioned that the tournament semifinals were scheduled for the next afternoon. The final round would be held on Sunday. Then some other Videomundo officials gave short speeches, and a children's chorus offered an excruciating rendition of what was billed as the "Official Videomundo Theme Song."

"Well, I'm raring to go," said Joe, as they exited the convention center. "Let's go back up to the room and play Hack Attack some more."

"I thought you'd had enough for the day," said Frank.

"I just got my second wind," Joe said. "I'm going to blow away the competition in the semifinals tomorrow."

"Wait a minute!" said Jason. "I *am* the competition!"

"Me, too," Nick Phillips said. "And I've got some plans to blow you away."

"Okay," said Joe, pointing at a familiar tall figure in the crowd. "As long as we all blow Bill Longworth away."

"I'll second that," said Nick. "I guess you've already met Longworth today."

"And how," said Joe. "I can't think of anybody I'd rather have eat my dust."

"I've had a couple of run-ins with Longworth in the past," said Nick. "I'm really looking forward to seeing him lose."

"One thing's for certain," said Frank. "This year's Mr. Congeniality Award isn't going to be won by last year's grand prize winner."

"So when are we going to eat?" asked Chet, as they reentered the main lobby of the hotel.

"Let's have room service send up some food," said Joe as they headed toward the elevator. "I'm serious about getting back to practice Hack Attack." He turned to Nick and Jason. "You guys want to join us?"

"Thanks," said Nick, "but I promised my brother I'd buy him some stuff from a little store down the street. Then I want to get back to my room for a little Hack Attack practice myself."

"Maybe I'll stop by a little later," said Jason. "I've got a couple of things I've got to take care of, too."

"See you later, then," said Joe, following Frank and Chet into the elevator.

"Which floor are we on again?" asked Chet, standing in front of the elevator's control panel.

"Tenth," said Joe. "We're in room 1034."

Chet punched the button. The elevator rose with a hum.

Joe flexed his hands in the air. "I'm telling you guys, I can feel the power in my fingers. I'm ready to take on the best Hack Attack players in the world."

"That's exactly what you'll be doing," said Frank. "Those guys don't look like slouches. Even Bill Longworth, as much as you hate to admit it, must be a great player if he could win last year's tournament."

"Last year," said Joe, "nobody really knew how to play Hack Attack yet. We've had a year to learn all the tricks and secrets."

"So has Bill Longworth," Chet reminded him.

"Well, that's true," said Joe, "but—"

Suddenly, there was a loud snapping noise from overhead. The elevator bumped violently, and the floor indicator flickered briefly at the number ten and then went dark.

Joe felt a lurch in the pit of his stomach and then experienced an odd sensation, as though he were actually floating in the air.

"We're falling!" he cried out. "The elevator cable's snapped! We're going to be killed!"

3 Back Doors

"What can we do?" shouted Chet in a panicked voice, as his stomach rose into his throat.

"Maybe," said Joe, shouting above the grinding noise as the falling elevator car bumped against the walls of the shaft, "there's an emergency—"

All at once the elevator stopped falling. Frank felt himself rise up off the floor. His head struck the elevator wall. Hard.

The three teenagers fell back to the floor of the car with a thud. The elevator seemed to bounce up and down for a moment as though it were a yo-yo balanced at the end of its string.

"—cable," muttered Joe, finishing his sentence even as he struggled to regain his senses.

27

"Oh, my head," said Frank, pulling himself up to a sitting position. He opened his eyes and was surprised to find that the lights in the elevator car were still on.

"I think I've lost my appetite," groaned Chet.

"It's a miracle!" said Joe. "It was worth the fall just to hear Chet say that."

"I almost lost my bag full of video games," said Chet.

"Now *that* would have been a disaster," said Joe.

"The emergency cable must have caught at the last second," said Frank. "Not a very good design, but I guess I shouldn't complain. We're still alive."

"Any landing you can walk away from is a good one," said Joe. "Now, how do we get out of here?"

"Pry the door open," said Frank, who was already fruitlessly pressing the Door Open button. "I hope we're not stuck between floors."

Joe stood and gripped the crack between the sliding doors, pulling outward. Slowly the doors began to slide open.

They were back on the ground floor, facing out into the lobby. Actually, the elevator was about one foot below the ground floor. Joe stepped up and onto the lobby carpet. Chet and Frank followed.

An anxious-looking security officer hurried

across the lobby to the bank of elevators. "What happened?" he asked. "Is the elevator out of order?"

"I guess you could say that," said Chet.

"I'm terribly sorry," said the security officer, staring through the half-opened doors into the elevator car. "This has never happened before. I assure you that these elevators are inspected on a regular basis."

Joe gave Frank a quizzical look. "Think it wasn't an accident?"

"Why would somebody want to kill us?" Frank asked.

"I don't know," said Joe. "Why would somebody want to swipe my bag of video game cartridges?"

"There's a profit in stealing video games," said Frank. "There's no profit in killing three teenagers. Besides, yours weren't the only cartridges that were stolen, not according to the story Nick Phillips told us."

"True," said Joe. "Maybe it's just a coincidence."

"But now that I think of it," said Frank, "maybe there is a—"

"—mystery here," Joe said, completing his brother's sentence.

The Hardys had solved quite a few cases in their lives, but Joe had hoped that this trip to New York City would serve as a vacation from their detective work. Joe and his brother were tired after their last case, *The Smoke Screen Mystery.* Catching an arsonist had proved to be hard work.

"Why do I always manage to get caught up in a case when I hang out with you guys?" asked Chet.

"I don't know," answered Joe. "You're just lucky, I guess."

"But seriously, Joe, I really think we should keep our eyes open," said Frank.

"Okay," agreed Joe.

"Well," said Chet, "are we going back to the room or not?"

"Yeah," said Joe. "But I think we'll take the stairs this time."

When they got back to the room, Chet insisted on playing Hack Attack for a few minutes himself, even though Joe wanted to practice for the semifinals the next day. Joe then decided that he needed a shower more than he needed game practice. When he came back from his shower, he found Chet staring dejectedly at the TV screen.

"What's the matter?" he asked.

"I keep getting zapped by that pack of dogs that runs across my path," moaned Chet.

"That's in the first screen of the game," said Joe.

"Don't rub it in," growled Chet.

Joe laughed. "My turn," he said, grabbing the game controller from Chet. "Is that your copy of Hack Attack in the machine or mine?"

"It's mine," said Chet. "Go ahead and play it. They're all the same."

Before Joe could sit down, there was a knock at the door. Frank opened it to find Jason Tanaka standing outside.

"Come on in, Jason," said Frank. "We were just settling down to another round of Hack Attack."

"I brought some other games, too," said Jason, holding up a paper bag. "I should think you'd be getting sick of Hack Attack by now."

"*I* am," said Frank.

"Well, I'm not," protested Joe. "But I guess we can look at the other games."

"Great," said Jason, sitting on the edge of one of the room's three beds. "Some of these games have really neat back doors built into them."

"Back doors?" asked Chet.

"Yeah," said Jason. "You know, secret ways to get extra lives, see special screens, that kind of thing."

"No, I don't know," said Joe. "Tell me more."

Jason pulled a cartridge out of his bag. "Here's the Battle of the Barbarians cartridge that I bought this afternoon. I've never played it before, but I've heard about some of the back doors that are in it. Let me show you."

31

He walked over to the television and pulled Chet's Hack Attack cartridge out of the game console. "Who does this belong to?"

"Me," said Chet, taking the cartridge from Jason. "I'd better keep it with the others." He put the Hack Attack cartridge back into the bag with his other games.

Jason plugged in the Battle of the Barbarians cartridge and turned the game console back on. A garish title screen, depicting a bloody sword with the words "Battle of the Barbarians" carved in stone in the background, appeared.

"Okay," said Jason, "this is the start-up screen. Now I have to press a certain sequence of buttons on the controller." He picked up the controller and started tapping. "Let's see . . . left, right, left, right, A button, B button, Start button."

Joe moved closer to the screen as the game began. Two heavily muscled barbarian warriors approached each other from opposite sides of the screen, one holding an oversized ax, the other a ridiculously long sword. Jason pointed at the number thirty in the upper left-hand corner of the screen.

"Ordinarily, you'd have three lives in this game. After you die three times, the game is over. But with that special back door I just triggered, you get thirty lives."

"You're kidding!" Joe exclaimed. "That's fantastic."

"Even better," said Jason, "the game gives you two continues. When the game ends, you get two chances to start over at the point where you left off. You'll get thirty lives for each continue, too, for a total of ninety lives."

"I love it," said Chet.

"If you can't get all the way through the game with ninety lives, you're a pretty pathetic player," Jason said. "Of course, *I'd* only need three lives, but not everybody is as good as I am."

"Think you're a pretty sharp player, don't you?" said Frank.

Jason laughed. "Sorry. I don't want to start sounding like Bill Longworth, but I *am* pretty good. I wouldn't be at this tournament if I weren't. Neither would Joe or Nick."

"Are there any more of these back doors?" asked Chet.

"There are one or two in almost every game," said Jason. "I know one other in this game. Let me show you."

He hit the reset button on the game console, and the start-up screen reappeared. Then he began pushing buttons on the controller again, muttering, "A, B, A, B, left, right, select, start. . . . Here we go."

Now the image of two large musical notes had appeared on the screen, and a catchy tune was coming out of the television speakers.

"What kind of game is this?" Frank asked. "Musical chairs?"

"No," Jason answered with a chuckle. "This is what's called a sound test mode. Some of these cartridges have a few dozen musical themes built into them, and the sound test mode lets you listen to all of them without having to play through the game."

He jabbed a button on the controller and the music changed. He jabbed another time, and it changed again.

"This is really weird," said Joe. "Where do these back doors come from, anyway? How do they get into the games?"

"The game programmers put them there," said Jason. "Usually, they help the programmers to test the game after they've finished writing it. Somebody has to play all the way through the game to make sure that there aren't any bugs in it. But not everybody is a good enough player to get all the way through the game, so they use the back doors to help them out. And the sound test mode helps them check the music, make sure it sounds right."

"How did you find out about these things?" asked Frank.

"It doesn't take long before game players learn where the back doors are in a game," said Jason. "And, once they find out, they tell other game

34

players. If you read the video game magazines, you'll see entire lists of them."

"Hey," said Joe, "are there any back doors in Hack Attack?"

Jason's face fell. "I wish I knew. Everybody assumes that there must be back doors in it someplace, but nobody's ever found one. Or, if they have, they're keeping their mouths shut about it."

"I thought you said it didn't take long for game players to find the back doors in a game," said Chet.

"Hack Attack is the exception," Jason replied. "I've been looking for back doors in that cartridge ever since it came out—*everybody's* been looking for back doors in Hack Attack—but we haven't found one yet. I'm still looking, though. Every time I practice the game, I try out different sequences of buttons on the controller, to see if I can hit the right one."

"Well, if you find one, let me know," said Joe. "It might come in handy at the tournament."

"Uh-uh," said Jason reprovingly. "That's a no-no! You don't use back doors in tournament play, or you'll be automatically eliminated from competition."

"Only if they catch me," said Joe. Jason gave him a dirty look. "Okay, okay, I'm just kidding," Joe said. "I'm too honest a guy for that." He sighed regretfully.

35

Chet shifted restlessly on his chair and asked, "You guys want to call room service?"

"Why don't we go out and eat?" said Jason. "I think you'll like that little diner down the block. You know, the one I tried to take you to before your games were stolen, Joe. It's casual and cheap."

"Sounds like my kind of place," said Joe.

"How's the food?" asked Frank.

"Not bad," answered Jason. "And there's a lot of it."

"Sounds like *my* kind of place," said Chet.

"Let's go," said Frank, picking up his keys and opening the door.

"Wait a minute," said Chet, hoisting his bag of video games. "I'd better put these in a safe place. If there's a video game thief loose in this hotel, I don't want these cartridges to get snatched."

"How about under the bed?" suggested Joe.

"Good idea," said Chet, shoving the bag out of sight. "The thief will never find them there."

"Not unless he spends ten seconds or so looking," said Joe with a laugh.

Chet frowned. "Maybe I'd better put them somewhere else."

Joe grabbed him by the neck and pulled him through the door. "Stop worrying! I can't believe that I've actually got to force you to leave the room and go eat!"

Five minutes later they were crossing the lobby

to the front door of the hotel. Suddenly, Joe patted the rear pocket of his pants.

"Whoops!" he said. "I left my wallet back in the room."

"That's okay," said Frank. "I'll pick up the tab. You buy me dinner tomorrow night."

"No way," said Joe. "You'll probably order the most expensive thing on the menu. I'll be right back, guys. Just wait for me here."

Joe hurried back to the elevator and returned to the tenth floor. As he walked down the hall to the room, he froze in his tracks. Something was wrong with the room.

The door was open. Someone was inside!

Joe tiptoed quietly to the door. Through the crack, he could see that the room had been ransacked, with drawers overturned on the floor and the sheets yanked off the bed. Cautiously, he started to open the door wider.

His hand was barely on the door handle when the door was abruptly whisked open by someone on the other side. Joe looked up to find himself face-to-face with a small man in a faded denim jacket—the same thief who had stolen his bag of video games that afternoon!

4 The Men from Omega

"Sorry," grunted the thief. "Guess I got the wrong room."

"Yeah, right," said Joe. "This is the room you wanted, and I know why."

Joe dived at the thief, but the small man bent over and rammed Joe in the stomach with his head. Joe was surprised by the move and didn't recover in time to grab the thief as he leapt past Joe and raced out the door. Seconds later, Joe hurried after him in pursuit.

"I've got to get that guy!" Joe said to himself.

Joe looked down the hallway and saw that the thief was headed straight for the door to the stairs. Joe immediately took after him. The thief hit the stairwell door running, knocking the door aside so hard that it slammed almost instantly closed. Joe hit it almost immediately after. As the door popped open, he could feel the impact in his bones. Joe grimaced in pain but was determined to continue his pursuit.

The sound of running footsteps echoed loudly in the stairwell as the thief headed down the stairs. Joe bounded down after him, taking the steps three at a time. The stairwell wound downward in short flights, each separated by a metal banister. Joe glanced down and saw that the thief was one flight ahead of him.

"Well, there's just one thing for me to do," Joe said to himself. He leapt over the banister and jumped down onto the thief's shoulders. The two of them fell down the stairs and collapsed in a heap on the next landing.

"Ow!" shouted the thief, who was pressed against the floor by Joe's bulk. "Are you trying to kill me?"

"Not a bad idea!" cried Joe. "What were you doing in our room?"

"Room service," snapped the thief. His fist flew out unexpectedly and clipped Joe in the jaw.

Stunned, Joe grabbed for the man, but it was too late. The thief was up and running again. By the time Joe was back on his feet, the thief had bolted out the stairwell door and down the carpeted hallway.

Joe was tempted to go after him, but something lying on the floor caught his eye.

Joe bent down and picked it up. It was a video game cartridge. "I don't believe it," Joe said aloud. "It's a Hack Attack cartridge!"

The thief must have dropped it, Joe thought. But why a Hack Attack cartridge? Did he steal this from our room?

Dismissing the idea of chasing the thief farther, Joe started back up the stairs to the tenth floor. As he headed toward his room, he saw Frank, Chet, and Jason coming up the hallway from the elevator.

"What happened to you?" asked Frank. "I thought you only came back for your wallet. What took so long?"

"We had a surprise visitor," answered Joe. "Come on into the room. I don't think you'll like what you see."

Frank stepped through the already open door. He looked around the room, surveying the damage. Clothes were strewn about, and the furniture was overturned.

"I don't believe this," Frank said, shaking his head. "Somebody's ransacked the place. What did he take?"

"This," said Joe, holding out the Hack Attack

cartridge. "As far as I can tell, it was the only thing he took."

"Who was it?" asked Frank. "The same guy who stole your cartridges earlier?"

"Yeah," confirmed Joe. "And I caught the weasel red-handed, right in this room. But unfortunately, he got away."

"Well, at least you got the cartridge back," commented Jason.

"Is that *my* Hack Attack cartridge?" asked Chet.

"I don't know," said Joe. "Is yours missing?"

"I'm not sure," Chet answered. "But I'm going to find out."

Chet found his video game bag lying on the floor to the side of the bed. The cartridges had been dumped out in a pile. He shuffled through them quickly.

"Yeah, it's missing," said Chet. "And it's the only cartridge that's gone from my batch."

"I don't get it," said Jason. "Why would somebody steal a Hack Attack cartridge? The tournament organizers are giving those things away as part of the publicity."

"They are?" said Chet. "You mean I didn't have to trade one of my cartridges for it?"

"Well, at least you didn't go out and buy one," said Frank. "The question is, what's so special about that Hack Attack cartridge that someone would steal it and leave all these other games behind?"

Frank shot a look at his brother, and Joe immediately knew what Frank was thinking. They definitely had another case to solve.

"Maybe it's not really a Hack Attack game in the cartridge," suggested Jason. "Maybe somebody removed the original ROM chip and put another one in."

"ROM chip?" asked Joe.

"Ready-Only-Memory. The electronic circuitry that stores the game program," said Jason.

"No, it's a Hack Attack game," said Chet. "I was playing it while Joe was in the shower."

"You never got past the opening screen," said Joe with a grin.

"I wish you'd quit reminding me of that," said Chet.

"Maybe we should play a little more of it," suggested Frank, "and make sure that it's legit."

"What we should do first," said Joe, "is call Steve Lewis and report this incident to him."

"Good idea," said Frank, picking up the telephone.

A few minutes later, Steve Lewis arrived with a security guard in tow. While Joe told him what had happened, the Videomundo representative listened intently.

"This is awful," Steve groaned. "Nothing like this happened at last year's tournament. I can't tell you how sorry I am that this had to happen to you twice."

"It's not your fault," said Joe. "And nothing really got stolen this time."

"Do you know why somebody would be stealing cartridges?" asked Frank. "I mean, aside from the obvious fact that they're worth money?"

Steve shrugged. "Maybe somebody's trying to hurt Videomundo's reputation. If they can ruin the tournament, they'll make us look pretty bad —and that could hurt our sales."

"Who'd want to hurt your sales?" asked Joe.

"Who do you think?" asked Steve rhetorically. "The competition, of course."

"Omega?" asked Jason, his eyebrows raised in surprise.

"I'm not naming names," said Steve. "Look, I'd better leave the theorizing to the police. The important thing is that the cartridges are okay and nobody got hurt. Oh, don't forget to stop by my office tomorrow, Joe, so I can arrange to get you some new games."

He started toward the door, then turned back. "About that cartridge of yours, Chet. If somebody wants it that badly, it might be better if you kept it in the hotel safe. I can arrange to have that done for you."

Chet clutched the cartridge to his chest. "Not on your life," he said. "I'm not letting this cartridge out of my sight again."

43

"Good enough," said Steve Lewis. He opened the door and followed the security officer into the hallway. "If you need me, you know my number."

"Right," said Joe. "I hope we *don't* need you again, but you'll hear from us if we do."

After Steve was gone, Frank said, "Maybe we should play that cartridge now."

"Good idea," said Joe, taking the cartridge from Chet and plugging it into the game machine. "I need the practice, anyway."

Joe played quickly through the first several screens of Hack Attack. Each was identical to the way his own copy of the game played.

"See any differences, Jason?" he asked.

"None whatsoever," Jason replied. "It looks like a standard Hack Attack cartridge."

"I guess I don't need to play any further," said Joe, turning off the television and removing the cartridge from the game console. "Here, Chet. You can have your cartridge back."

"Thanks," said Chet, taking the cartridge and slipping it inside his shirt. "I'm not letting this off my body."

"Even when you sleep?" asked Frank.

"And shower?" asked Joe.

"Never," said Chet. "I'm protecting it with my life."

"I'm not sure that showering would be good for the ROM chip," said Jason.

"I'll be careful," said Chet with a chuckle. "Now, are we going to dinner?"

"Yes," said Frank. "And maybe this time we'll actually make it."

The teens walked out of the hotel room. But before closing the door, Frank stopped and called Joe back inside.

"Hey, Joe. Come here for a minute," Frank said quietly.

"Yeah, sure. We'll be right back, guys," Joe said to Jason and Chet.

"What's up?" asked Joe as he stepped inside the room and closed the door behind him.

"It looks like we're about to investigate something here, but it also looks like Jason's along for the ride."

"What are you getting at?" asked Joe.

"Well, even though Jason seems like a nice guy, we really don't know if we can trust him."

"But, Frank," Joe said, "you don't think he's involved with the thefts? Remember, he was with you when I found the thief in our room. Unless he's a magician, he couldn't possibly have been in two places at one time."

"True, but let's still be careful," responded Frank. "We've been fooled before. Now, let's get something to eat."

Frank and Joe left the room and rejoined their friends. But they only made it as far as the hotel lobby. Suddenly, Joe grabbed Frank by one shoulder and pointed to a bunch of men in dark suits, who were clustered in one corner of the room.

"It's those guys from Omega," said Joe. "What are they doing here again? Remember what Steve Lewis said about the competition a few minutes ago?"

"Maybe they want to see the tournament," said Frank.

"That's exactly why they're here," agreed Jason. "They want to track Videomundo's every move."

Joe watched closely as two of the Omega men split off from the group and headed toward the back entrance of the lobby. One of them had wide shoulders and a ruddy face, with graying hair. The other was tall and skinny, with a pale complexion. He was carrying a large brown box in his arms.

"I wonder what's in the box?" Joe asked. "That looks pretty suspicious to me."

"Maybe it's his dinner," suggested Chet. "Maybe I'll ask him if he wants to split it, since it looks like we're never going to make it to that diner."

"I'm going to follow this guy," said Joe. "Anybody want to come with me?"

"Not me," said Chet. "I'm going to go eat."

"Oh, okay," said Frank. "I'll come along. But I'm not sure it's such a good idea."

"Mind if I join you?" said Jason. "This looks like fun."

"Terrific," said Chet. "When am I going to learn not to hang around you two detectives? Count me in."

The four teenagers silently slipped into the back corridor, where the Omega representatives had gone. Frank could see the two dark-suited men about twenty yards in front of them, heading toward a distant doorway. Moments later, they opened the door and stepped through.

"I think that back exit leads into the alleyway near the hotel's loading dock," Jason said in a low tone.

Moments later, Frank reached the door and pushed it open slightly. In the alley, he saw the two Omega representatives standing behind a large black delivery truck. The rear door of the truck was open, and a burly man in work clothes, who Frank guessed was the driver, stood inside the back of the truck, talking to the men in suits. The burly man was about thirty-five years old, had close-cropped black hair, and looked extremely muscular.

"Now what?" asked Frank. "You think there's something suspicious about this?"

"I'm not sure," said Joe. "I want to see what's in that box."

The burly man took the box from the Omega

47

representative and hoisted it into the back of the truck. Then he reached inside the box and pulled something out.

It was a Videomundo game cartridge.

"That's it!" said Joe, his voice rising. "It's one of my stolen cartridges!"

5 The Japanese Connection

Joe started to push the door all the way open, but Frank grabbed it and held it back.

"Are you positive that's a Videomundo cartridge?" he asked. "Maybe it's an Omega cartridge."

"That's definitely a Videomundo cartridge," Jason said. "I can tell the difference even at this distance. The Videomundo cartridges are much larger than the Omega cartridges."

"I'm telling you, that's a stolen cartridge," Joe said to his brother.

"But how can you be sure they stole that

49

cartridge, or that they even stole it from you?" Chet asked.

"Well, there's just one way to find out," Joe said as he pushed open the door. "I'm going to talk with these guys."

"Wait a second, Joe," said Frank.

But Joe ignored his brother and strode out onto the loading dock and jumped to the alley below. "Hey!" he shouted at the three men. "What do you think you're doing?"

The two men in dark suits turned to Joe and looked at him as though they thought he had gone crazy. "Are you talking to us?" the tall man asked.

"That's right," said Joe. "You're from Omega games, aren't you?"

"Yes, we are," said the man with the graying hair. "If you don't mind, we were just leaving. It's getting late."

"I just want to know what you're doing with that box full of Videomundo cartridges," said Joe.

"That box?" said the man on the left, pointing into the truck.

"Yeah," said Joe. "That box."

"We purchased these from representatives of Videomundo," said the man on the right. "It was a perfectly legitimate transaction."

"Then why are you sneaking out the back way?" Joe persisted.

50

"We're not sneaking," the man on the left said. "We're just loading these into the truck. They'll be taken back to our offices. We have several boxes full of games in the truck."

"Several boxes?" said Joe. "That's probably about how many games were stolen today."

"I'm not sure I know what you're talking about," said the man on the right. "Now, if you'll excuse us, we have to be leaving."

"Wait a minute!" Joe exclaimed. "You can't just leave here with all these stolen—"

Frank walked up behind Joe and placed a hand on his brother's shoulder. "Joe, we have no proof that those are stolen cartridges. I think we'd better look for more evidence first." He turned to the Omega representatives. "I'm sorry about this. My brother is a little hot under the collar. There have been some thefts recently."

"But they've got the motive," Joe protested. "You heard what Steve Lewis said about the competition trying to ruin Videomundo's reputation!"

"Calm down, Joe," said Frank. "That guy's bigger than you are."

The Omega representatives climbed into the cab of the truck. The burly man in the back of the truck joined them, and the truck pulled away. At Frank's urging, Joe followed the others back into the building.

51

"Now I've lost my appetite," said Joe.

"Well, I've still got mine," said Chet. "Are we going to eat or not?"

"It's getting too late," said Frank. "There are some vending machines in a room next to the stairwell. We'll grab some sandwiches there. You can show us the diner in the morning, Jason, for breakfast."

"It's a deal," said Jason.

"I'm glad I brought lots of change," said Chet.

The next morning Frank, Joe, Jason, and Chet met in the hotel lobby. Jason led them down the block and paused below a pink neon sign that read "King's Diner." The shiny chrome exterior looked inviting. Frank opened the front door and led the group to a plush red leather booth and sat down. Across the aisle, Frank's eye caught two men sitting at a long counter, sipping hot coffee and sinking their teeth into bagels piled high with cream cheese. Frank's stomach began to rumble. A few seconds later, a uniformed waitress named Darlene, who wore her blond hair pinned under a tight net, came over to the table and took their order.

"Finally," said Chet. "I'm ready for some serious food."

"You had three vending machine sandwiches last night." Joe reminded him.

"Not to mention the two slices of vending machine pizza," added Frank.

"I said serious food," Chet protested, "not a late-night snack."

"I'm really up for the semifinals," said Jason with a smile. "I went back to my room last night and racked up my highest score yet on Hack Attack!"

"How high was it?" asked Joe.

"Six million, seven hundred thousand, five hundred and eight points," said Jason. "Have you done better?"

Joe cleared his throat. "I, uh, don't keep records."

"You ought to," said Jason. "When you play as well as we do, your only real competition is yourself."

"How did you get involved in video games, Jason?" asked Frank.

"Four years ago, I was visiting Japan with my parents," he said. "I bought a Videomundo console over there and brought it back with me."

"I thought that the VGC had only been on sale for three years," said Joe. "That's what Steve Lewis said in his speech yesterday."

"That's true in the United States," said Jason, "but it came out two years earlier in Japan. By the time I bought mine, the video game craze was already in full swing in Japan."

"That's right," said Frank. "You said it started over there."

"Well, it didn't entirely," said Jason. "Actually, the first video games were developed in America in the early 1970s, and the first home game machines appeared here about half a decade later. But the craze fell apart in the early 1980s, and sales of game cartridges plunged. By the middle of the decade, most American companies didn't want anything to do with video games.

"But Videomundo changed that in Japan. They were a small company with a couple of coin-operated games in the arcades when they decided to bring out the Videomundo Game Console. It didn't sell very well at first—until they released Hack Attack. The game caught on almost immediately, and for a while they could hardly make enough of the consoles to meet the demand."

"Wait a minute," said Joe. "That means that Hack Attack came out in Japan years ago. I thought it was only two years old. I hadn't even *heard* of it before the big tournament last year."

"Most video games for the VGC come out in Japan before they're released here in the States," said Jason. "Hack Attack was around in Japan for more than two years before it got here. It's still a best-seller over there."

"You mean there are Japanese video games that we've never seen in this country?" asked Chet.

54

"Sure," said Jason. "Plenty of them. Most of those games that Steve Lewis showed at the opening ceremonies last night have been available in Japan for months. They've already got The Adventures of Bobbity Babbit Four in Japan, while we're only just starting to play number three in this country."

"Boy," said Joe, "it makes me want to take a trip to the Orient!"

"I hope to take another trip there this summer," said Jason, "and buy as many video games as I can afford!"

"You'll have to show them to me!" said Joe.

"And me, too!" added Chet.

"It's a deal," said Jason. "Of course, I know about fifty other guys who want to look at them, too."

The waitress returned with several plates full of food. Chet's was stacked high with pancakes, eggs, and sausages.

"Tell me about this Omega Corporation," said Frank to Jason. "After what happened in back of the hotel last night, I'm curious to know more about those guys."

"There's not a lot to tell," said Jason. "Like Videomundo, they're a Japanese corporation with an American branch. They brought out the Omega Super System in Japan in imitation of the VGC, but it's never really caught on the way Videomundo's machine has. There aren't as many games for it, and most game players agree that the games that *do* exist aren't as good."

"Do you think Omega would try to sabotage Videomundo's tournament?" asked Joe, pausing briefly before stuffing a slice of bacon into his mouth.

"It doesn't seem likely," said Jason. "But maybe I'm just being naive. Come to think of it, I have read in some of the video game magazines that the Omega Corporation has been accused of shady business practices."

"What sort of practices?" asked Frank.

"Oh, strong-arming retailers into carrying their products, industrial espionage, that sort of thing," said Jason.

"Industrial espionage?" Joe raised an eyebrow.

Jason shrugged. "As far as I know, both Videomundo and Omega like to spy on each other. They probably have contacts in each other's organizations who get them advance copies of new games before they come out. I've heard that a lot of companies do that. It gives them a chance to develop their own games in imitation, in case the other guy has something that looks like it'll be really popular."

"Isn't that against the law?" asked Frank.

"Not necessarily," said Jason. "The methods the companies use to obtain the cartridges aren't exactly illegal, and they're careful to avoid copyright problems. The games are never direct copies."

"Hmmm," said Frank thoughtfully. "I think I might want to check out this Omega Corporation a little more thoroughly."

"What did I tell you?" Joe added. "Those guys last night looked pretty suspicious to me!"

After breakfast, the four strolled back to the hotel. The tournament would be starting shortly, and both Joe and Jason were ready to go.

Joe was looking forward to playing in the tournament even though he was feeling the pre-game jitters in his stomach. "I can't wait," he said. "I don't think I've ever been this psyched about a competition, even in a football game."

"I don't play football, but I know what you mean," Jason said as he and the others paused at the end of a block. "I've been in training for this thing all year."

Suddenly, there was a screeching of tires. Frank turned to see a large black car pull up to the curb and a bulky man in a jogging suit jump out of the backseat. A second man sat behind the steering wheel, racing the motor. The man in the jogging suit ran up behind Chet and grabbed him under the arms in a wrestling hold.

"Hey!" shouted Chet. "What are you doing?"

"Yeah," added Joe. "Let go of my friend!"

Ignoring Joe's plea, the man tugged Chet toward the automobile and thrust him violently into the backseat. Joe rushed after him, but the bulky man knocked Joe aside with a quick swing of a massive arm. Stunned, Joe staggered back across the sidewalk.

As Frank and his two companions watched helplessly, the car pulled away from the curb with Chet still in the backseat, yelling for help!

6 Let the Games Begin!

"They've got Chet!" Joe yelled. "We've got to catch them!"

"How?" asked Jason. "We don't have a car."

"We'll flag a cab," said Frank as he stepped off the curb and waved at a bright yellow taxi passing by. It sped past as though it hadn't even seen Frank.

"Great. We've got no time to lose," Joe said, looking down the block at the car with Chet in it, which had stopped behind several cars at a red light.

Finally a cab came to a halt. Joe hopped in the

front seat, and Frank and Jason climbed into the back.

"Follow that car!" Joe shouted, pointing at the rapidly vanishing black car that had taken Chet away.

"Are you putting me on?" asked the cabdriver. "What is this, a James Bond movie?"

"We're serious, sir," said Frank from the backseat. "Our friend's been kidnapped by the guys in that car, and we've got to stop them."

With a scowl on his face, the driver looked at Frank through the rearview mirror. "I hope you're paying for this in advance."

"Here!" said Joe, throwing a couple of bills onto the seat. "Is that enough?"

"It's a start," said the driver. With a squeal of tires, he pulled away from the curb and started in the direction of the black car.

Two blocks ahead, the black car made a right turn and vanished briefly. But when the cab turned the corner, the black car was only one block ahead, held up by another red light and thick traffic on a cross street.

"We've got them!" Joe yelled. "Let us out here!"

"Be my guest," said the cabbie, pulling to the curb and letting the three of them climb out. "I don't suppose you want your change."

"Keep it for a tip," said Frank, as he slammed the door and raced after the others.

As Joe ran up behind the black car, two men jumped out. One was the bulky man in the jogging suit, the other was an even larger man in polyester pants and a knit shirt. Chet burst out of the back door a second later. The driver of the car immediately behind the black car began honking his horn loudly at the stationary vehicle.

"He's got my Hack Attack cartridge!" Chet yelled, pointing at the man in the jogging suit.

Joe raced to his side. "Let him keep it. At least you're okay."

"No way!" said Chet. "I want my cartridge back!"

Joe watched as Chet took off after the bulky man.

"Frank," Joe called to his brother, "I'm going to help Chet get the big guy. See if you can nab the other one." With that, Joe took off in pursuit of the thief.

Up ahead, Joe saw the bulky man weaving his way through the thick traffic. It looked as if he was headed for the opposite side of the street. A large chartered bus was parked against the curb, and for a moment the thief hesitated, trying to decide how to get around it.

"Go that way!" yelled Joe, motioning for Chet to go around one end of the bus in pursuit of the cartridge thief. Joe veered off in the opposite direction, driving the thief back toward Chet. In desperation, the thief flattened himself against the ground and rolled underneath the carriage of the bus. But when he emerged on the other side, he found Joe and Chet coming at him from opposite directions.

"Gotcha!" cried Chet, as Joe raced up behind the thief and grabbed him by the shoulders. "I want my cartridge back!"

Chet wrestled the cartridge out of the thief's grasp as Joe held the bulky man immobile. "Okay!" snapped the thief. "You got your cartridge back. Now let go of me!"

"Sorry," said Joe. "We're calling the police. You kidnapped my friend and stole his property. Where I come from, that's against the law."

"Yeah?" said the thief. "Well, this is New York City, and kidnapping the tourists is just one of our customs."

"Sure it is," said Joe. Chet flagged a passerby and asked her to call the police from a nearby pay phone. Ten minutes later, a police cruiser pulled up. By that time, Frank and Jason had appeared with the other kidnapper in tow. After hearing the story of what had happened, the two officers took the two men into custody.

"Whew!" said Jason, after the excitement was over. "Does trouble like this follow you guys wherever you go?"

"Pretty much," said Frank. "We like it this way. We have a low threshold of boredom."

"Whoa!" said Joe, looking at his watch. "We're going to be late for the tournament! We'd better get back to the convention center!"

"Want to take a cab?" asked Jason.

"Let's walk this time," said Joe.

Frank and Chet settled back in the VIP seats that Joe had secured for them in the convention center arena, directly overlooking the wide stage where the Hack Attack tournament players were seated at their specially designed video game stations. Frank leaned forward in his seat and studied the stage. Each gaming station included a video game console, a computer monitor with a crisp color image, a Hack Attack cartridge provided by the tournament organizers, and a chair to sit on. Frank looked around for his brother.

"There's Joe," said Frank, pointing to where his brother sat at his video game station, clutching a game controller in his hand.

"And Jason," added Chet.

"And Nick Phillips," said Frank.

"We know so many people in this tournament now," said Chet, "that it's hard to know who to root for."

"It's no problem for me," said Frank. "I may like Jason and Nick, but I'm still rooting for my brother. It'll be nice to have an extra fifty thousand dollars in the family."

"Yeah," said Chet. "And you could share some of it with your friends."

Frank leaned back and looked up at the ceiling of the arena, where brightly colored banners announced the tournament and advertised Videomundo Corporation products. The seats were filled with onlookers young and old. Near the stage, Frank saw a couple of television crews setting up their equipment. Reporters and corporate executives milled around the stage area, waiting for the tournament to begin.

"Ladies and gentlemen," said Steve Lewis, speaking into a microphone on a small podium at one end of the stage. "I'd like to welcome you back to the semifinals of the Second Annual National Hack Attack Tournament. As you know, the players in this tournament were chosen in a series of local competitions sponsored by the Videomundo Corporation. There will be two dozen players competing today for the right to return in tomorrow's finals. However, only the top four players will be able to return tomorrow. So, as you can imagine, there is a lot of pressure on these young men and women to perform at their best this afternoon. I'd like you to give all of them a great big round of applause!"

The audience responded with a hearty cheer. Frank and Chet stood and clapped loudly, shouting Joe's name and whistling. When Steve Lewis read off the names of the individual players, they clapped and whistled again as Joe's name was announced.

"Go, Joe!" Chet yelled for extra measure. "You can do it!"

"And now," Steve Lewis went on, "as they like to say at the Olympics, let the games begin!"

As the playing started, Frank and Chet watched the multiple television screens suspended from the ceiling come alive. Each screen was divided into four images, with each image showing the picture that one of the Hack Attack players was seeing on his or her own monitor. The player's name was superimposed over the image, so that the onlookers could follow the games of their favorite contestants.

At first, Frank noticed that each screen showed the same image: a busy city street, not unlike the one in front of the hotel, as viewed from above. A tiny red cab waited at the curb to pick up a passenger. In the upper right-hand corner of the screen was a stylized signpost reading New York City.

Then, as Frank watched, a tiny pedestrian walked up to the cab, opened the door, and climbed inside. On each screen, the name of a city appeared in a rectangle in the lower right-hand corner, but on each screen the city was different.

"Joe got San Francisco," said Frank. "That's a tough one."

"Yeah," said Chet. "He'll have to drive all the way across the country for that one, unless he gets the wings. But it's also a larger fare, so he'll get more points. So in a way, he lucked out."

"Jason got New Orleans," said Frank.

"Yeah," said Chet. "And Nick got Atlanta. Both of those are easier, but they'll have to pull more fares to make up for the lower points."

On each screen, a taximeter on the right-hand side of the screen began ringing up points. Frank looked at Joe's screen. His brother's cab was racing at a high speed toward the southwest limits of the city. At random intervals, cars veered into his path, pedestrians and dogs wandered into the street, fire hydrants burst in colorful sprays of water, and other obstacles strewed themselves in the taxi's path. But Joe managed to avoid them all without any noticeable effort.

"Of course," said Frank, "this is the early part of the game. It gets tougher as it goes."

"You bet," said Chet. "Joe could play this part in his sleep."

After a few minutes, Joe's taxicab left the city and began meandering across open countryside, where the only obstacles were occasional stray cows and rock slides. Many of the roads on the screen led to dead ends, but Frank noticed that Joe stayed on a carefully memorized path that led to San Francisco in the minimum possible time.

"Uh-oh," said Chet as he noticed a sudden

66

flurry of activity on Joe's screen. "It's the Attack of the Killer Sports Cars! Now things are going to get tough!"

Frank sat on the edge of his seat as a half dozen sleek black automobiles materialized from the corners of the screen and zeroed in on Joe's taxi. Within seconds, one of the black cars had positioned itself directly behind Joe's rear bumper and began zooming in for the kill.

"What are you going to do now, Joe?" Frank asked.

"Use the oil slick!" Chet urged.

Sure enough, a rainbow-hued pool of liquid appeared directly behind Joe's cab. The black car plowed into it at full speed and began spinning wildly, skidding back and forth until it hit a bridge abutment and disappeared in a flash of colored particles.

"I'm not sure that's environmentally sound," said Frank, sliding back down in his seat.

"I don't think Joe cares about that right now," said Chet. "Whoops, here comes another one." He pointed at a second black automobile racing toward Joe's cab from the top of the screen.

"Oh, no!" Frank cried. "A head-on collision! Joe, you'd better do something fast!"

7 The Final Four

Frank held his breath, but he knew that Joe could get out of this tight spot.

Sure enough, the cab came to a squealing stop, but another black car immediately appeared from behind.

"He's surrounded again," said Chet. "Like I told him yesterday, he'd better use the laser beam."

"This taxicab is really well equipped," said Frank admiringly.

Frank's eyes grew wide as a fountain of yellow and orange light rays sprayed out of the cab in all directions, vaporizing the two black cars a split second before they could collide with the cab.

"Wahoo!" trumpeted Chet. "Three down and three to go!"

"And here come numbers four, five, and six," said Frank, pointing at the screen. "All at the same time."

Frank's prediction was right. The remaining three cars were closing in quickly, from three different sides, on the taxi. Joe tapped the controller and started to swing the cab through a tight U-turn, but before he could reverse direction, the sound of gushing water came out of the television's speakers. Directly behind the taxi, a torrent of water burst out of a lake and flowed across the highway, cutting off Joe's retreat.

"Flash flood!" said Chet. "The dam's burst!"

"What's he going to do now?" asked Frank.

"I don't know," answered Chet. "He only had one laser beam, and he won't get another one until the bonus round. Looks like he's going to lose this cab."

All at once, powerful energy rays pulsed in from all sides of the screen, forming a star burst of light on the road ahead.

"A warp zone!" cried Chet. "Dynamite! Joe can warp right out of the path of those cars. And if he's lucky, it'll warp him all the way to San Francisco!"

Joe drove straight into the warp zone, and for a moment the screen dissolved into a rainbow-colored spiral. Then the cab reappeared in the middle of another city.

The signpost in the upper right-hand corner read "NOME, ALASKA."

"Uh-oh," said Chet. "Bad luck. Nome is even farther from San Francisco than New York. And he'll have to cross the glacier zone to get there. Oh well, at least he didn't get pulverized by those sports cars."

Frank laced his hands behind his head and leaned back.

"Better get comfortable," he said. "This is going to be a long ride."

Over the next few hours, Frank watched Joe and his fellow Hack Attack players fight off alien invaders, enemy submarines, tornadoes in Kansas, earthquakes in California, and exploding peaches in Georgia—all while driving passengers from one destination to another to earn the fares that gave them more and more points.

After a half hour, the first player had dropped out. His cab got lost somewhere in the depths of the Carlsbad Caverns in New Mexico and eventually ran out of gas. Approximately every ten minutes after that, another contestant had called it quits, until only Joe, Jason, Nick, and Bill were still playing.

"Well, it looks like we know who the finalists are," said Frank.

"Go, Joe!" shouted Chet. "Show 'em you've got what it takes!"

When the last games finally ended, the players stood up wearily and sat at the edge of the stage, waiting for their standings to be announced.

Joe wiped the sweat from his forehead with the back of his hand and said to Jason, who sat beside him, "I'm exhausted, but boy, was that a blast!"

Jason nodded and said, "And to top it off, we're both finalists."

What a great day, Joe thought. His ears perked up as Steve Lewis remounted the podium and read the results.

"In fourth place," Steve said, "Nick Phillips.

"In third place, Joe Hardy.

"In second place, Bill Longworth.

"In first place, Jason Tanaka."

There was a long burst of applause as the finalists stood one by one and took their bows.

"I guess Jason really is as good as he thinks he is," said Frank.

"Joe's gonna be mad," added Chet. "Coming in after Bill Longworth."

"At least he's in the finals," said Frank. "He'll have his chance for revenge tomorrow. Come on. Let's meet Joe backstage."

When they reached the floor of the arena, the younger Hardy was standing next to the stage, looking as though he had just run a marathon.

71

"Boy, am I wiped out," said Joe. "I've never played that hard in my life. Even at football."

Jason walked up with a smile. "That was great!" he exclaimed. "I thought that game would never end! I just kept racking up point after point! It was easy!"

"Easy for you, maybe," said Joe.

"Hey, Tanaka!" snapped a familiar voice. Jason turned to see Bill Longworth standing behind him.

"Hey, yourself, Bill," said Jason. "You turned in a good game. You almost beat me."

"I don't know what you were up to, Tanaka," said Longworth, ignoring Jason's comment, "but you must have been cheating. I played as well as I've ever played, and you still got a better score. Something's wrong here."

"Huh?" said Jason. "What are you talking about?"

"Get off Jason's case, Longworth!" Joe said, defending his friend. "You beat *me*. Isn't that good enough?"

Longworth ignored Joe's comment. "I'm going to blow you away tomorrow, Tanaka," he continued. "Just you wait and see. And if I catch you cheating somehow, using back doors or something to win this game, I'm going to see that you get what's coming to you!"

The lanky game player turned on his heel and

stormed away, leaving Joe, Jason, Chet, and Frank staring after him in astonishment.

"I didn't think that jerk's attitude problem could get any worse," said Joe, "but I think it just did."

"Ignore him, Jason," advised Frank. "He's just trying to psych you out, get the edge on you in tomorrow's finals."

"All he's doing is making me more anxious to beat him," said Jason. "And I have no doubt that I will."

"Hey, look! There's Nick Phillips," said Joe. "Howdy, Nick! Good work in the tournament!"

Nick wandered over to where his friends were standing, a bleak look on his face. "I did lousy," he said. "I came in fourth."

"Fourth out of twenty-four contestants," Frank reminded him. "That's pretty good in my book. And you made the cutoff for the finals."

"Not good enough," said Nick angrily. "I'm going to lose. What a stupid thing to do!"

"Losing isn't stupid," said Joe. "You're doing your best. And you still have a chance to win."

"Yeah," said Nick, walking away. "Thanks a lot."

"What's eating him?" asked Chet.

"What's eating everybody?" said Joe. "I thought we were all here to have fun. Everybody's taking this thing so seriously!"

73

"Maybe we all should get our minds off this tournament," said Frank, "and worry about the mystery of Chet's ever-popular cartridge. Do you have it with you, Chet?"

"Of course I do," replied Chet, patting his jacket pocket.

"Let me have it," said Frank.

"No," said Chet. "I told you, I'm protecting it with my life."

"We won't solve the mystery that way," said Frank. "I just want to examine the cartridge to see if there's anything odd about it."

"I've got a better idea," said Jason. "Let me examine it. I'm an expert on Hack Attack and video games in general. I'll play the cartridge in my room later. If there's anything at all different about that cartridge, I'll find out what it is."

"Well," said Chet, "if you promise to be careful with it." He pulled out the cartridge and handed it to Jason.

"Believe me," said Jason, "nobody respects video game cartridges more than I do."

"Just don't let anybody get it away from you," said Frank.

"Don't worry," said Jason. "The people who want this cartridge will think that Chet still has it. I'll be safe . . . but Chet won't."

"Oh, great," said Chet. "Maybe I should wear a sign that says No Hack Attack cartridges on this human being."

"Let's get back to the hotel," said Joe. "I think they're closing up the arena."

The four teenagers trooped back down the hallway and into the lobby of the hotel. Just as they neared the front door, Joe spotted two familiar figures. A bulky man in a jogging suit and an even larger man in a knit shirt walked in from the street outside.

Joe froze in his tracks. Chet gulped in astonishment.

It was the two men who had kidnapped Chet that very morning!

8 Industrial Espionage

"What are you guys doing here?" Joe demanded angrily.

"Yeah," said Chet. "You're supposed to be in jail. We're going to call the cops!"

"Ha!" laughed the man in the knit shirt. "The cops can't touch us. We're out on bail."

"Yeah," added the man in the jogging suit. "It's all nice and legal. We're just minding our own business."

"Just what kind of business is that?" Joe inquired as he planted himself in front of the man.

Frank grabbed Joe before the encounter became too dangerous. "They may have a point,

76

Joe," he said. "If they're out on bail, there's nothing we can do."

"But they kidnapped Chet just a few hours ago!" Joe retorted.

"I didn't say it was fair," said Frank, "but it may be legal."

"Sorry to run off," said the man in the knit shirt, "but we've got places to go and people to see. Catch you kids later!"

"I hope that you don't mean that literally," snapped Joe, as the two men walked away into the hotel.

"What do you suppose they're doing here?" asked Jason.

"I don't know, but I'm going to ask Steve Lewis about it," said Joe.

Joe led the others to the Videomundo representative's office. Peering into the office through a half-opened door, Joe saw that Steve was talking on the phone. Steve looked up, saw Joe, and motioned for him to enter and sit down. After Steve hung up the phone, Joe explained what had happened to Chet and that the two kidnappers were presently in the hotel. Joe waited for Steve's response.

Steve leaned back in his chair. "After what you've just told me, Joe, I'm surprised that the two men would be out on bail so soon. I'm going to give my contact at the police department a call. Excuse me," he said, reaching for the phone.

After a few minutes, Steve hung up the phone. "It looks like what they told you was true," he said, shaking his head. "Someone posted bail. It's all fair and square."

"Who posted the bail?" asked Joe.

"No one knows," Steve replied. "Apparently it was done anonymously. And in cash."

"This is incredible," muttered Joe. "Those two guys tried to kidnap my friend, and now they're back on the streets again."

"It doesn't mean they can get away with trying it again," said Steve. "If they try to harm you, call the police."

"That didn't seem to do us much good," Joe said.

"And they're probably still after my Hack Attack cartridge," added Chet.

"Are you sure you don't want to put the cartridge in the hotel safe?" asked Steve. "The offer still stands."

"Thanks, but no thanks," said Chet. "Besides, Jason's got the cartridge now."

"And I doubt that anybody will think to snatch it from me," added Jason.

"Okay," said Steve. "All I can say is, be careful. I'm afraid I've got to get back to work now. With the finals coming up tomorrow, I've got lots of arrangements to make."

"We understand," said Frank.

"Yeah," said Joe. "Thanks for all the help, Steve. You've been great."

"What now?" said Frank, after they left the office.

"Time to do some more investigating," said Joe.

"Maybe we should follow those two guys," said Chet.

"Not a bad idea," said Frank, "but they seem to have disappeared. Maybe we'll pick them up again later."

"We can check out those Omega guys," said Joe. "I still don't trust them."

"I haven't seen them around since the tournament," said Frank. "I noticed they were there in force, but they left immediately afterward."

"You could try their corporate offices," suggested Jason. "They're right here in Manhattan."

"Great!" said Joe. "Do you have their address?"

"No, but it's in the phone book," Jason said.

"Let's go," said Frank. "I want to talk to these guys. You coming along, Jason?"

"I don't think so," said Jason. "I'm ready to play some more Hack Attack up in my room."

"I'd think you'd be sick of Hack Attack," said Chet, "after the tournament."

"Oh, no," said Jason. "I'm more excited about it than ever. Plus, the competition is going to be pretty stiff tomorrow."

"I'm glad to see you haven't underestimated the powers of your opponents," Joe said with mock pride.

"We'll see you later, Jason," Frank said, "and we'll give your regards to Omega."

Frank checked the address of the Omega headquarters in a Manhattan phone book at the hotel desk. Omega's office was located in midtown Manhattan, so Frank decided that they'd better take the subway. He consulted the subway map he carried in his pocket and found out that they needed to take the F train. With Chet and Joe, he walked to the F train stop. The group purchased tokens, walked through the turnstile, and headed for the uptown side. A few minutes later, the train arrived, and the three rode it to the Lexington Avenue station, where they got off. They walked south on Lexington, checking the numbers on the tall buildings, and then crossed the street.

"Here we are, Omega corporate headquarters," said Frank, looking up at a huge, black glass building.

Frank led the group inside, checked the directory in the lobby, and found that the Omega Corporation occupied the top two floors of the building. The three teenagers took the elevator to their destination and stepped out into a large foyer. Frank looked around to see a receptionist seated at a glossy black desk. Contemporary oil paintings hung on the wall behind her, alternating with posters showing the company's latest games.

"Hi," said Frank. "We're big fans of your company and just love playing your games. We were wondering if we could see your offices and take a look at how the games are created."

"Certainly," said the receptionist. She picked up the phone and pressed a button. "We're always happy to give tours to our customers. If you'll wait a moment, I'll have Mr. Gensher show you around."

A few minutes later, Frank saw a young man in a gray suit heading their way. He stopped in front of them and introduced himself as Mr. Gensher. The boys introduced themselves in turn, and Gensher ushered them into the offices.

He gestured at the doors along the hallway. "These are just our corporate offices," he said. "I'm sure you're not interested in what they're doing. It's just a lot of paperwork, I assure you."

"Paperwork?" Joe whispered to Frank. "Or spy work?"

"Now, in here," he said, pointing to a door at the end of the hallway, "is something I think you'll find much more exciting."

He led them into a large room where rows of video game machines were lined up, one after another.

"Wow," Joe said as he looked around the room,

"I could have a *blast* in this room." Joe noticed that each video game machine was attached to a monitor and each seemed to be running a different game. And at each machine sat a young man or woman holding a game controller and playing a game.

"This is our play-testing room," said Gensher. "This is where we make sure that there are no bugs in our games and that each is as exciting as we can possibly make it."

"Wow," said Chet. "I could live in this place."

"It's really neat," said Joe. "How about showing us a few of the games?"

"Of course," said Gensher. "I'm afraid I can't give or sell you copies of the games, since they're not even on the market yet and I'm sure our competitors would love to get their hands on them. But you're welcome to look at them. And be sure to tell all your friends about them."

"Oh, we will," said Chet.

"Now, this game," said Gensher, indicating one of the monitors, "is our hot new summer release. It's called Phasers and Phantoms."

While Gensher talked, Frank slipped quietly back through the door they had entered and into the hallway. He peered cautiously into several rooms but saw nothing out of the ordinary. Then, at the other end of the corridor, he found an empty room piled high with video game cartridges.

He stepped inside. The cartridges were strewn about the room in a disorganized array. On several tables, video game consoles from both Omega and Videomundo were noisily playing games all by themselves, with nobody around to tend them.

Frank picked up a few of the cartridges. Some of them were games from Omega, but most of them were by Videomundo. He recognized several titles from Steve Lewis's presentation at the opening ceremonies of the tournament. They were the games that Videomundo would be releasing that summer. Other games had titles that he didn't even recognize, and several had titles written in Japanese. There were also several Hack Attack cartridges.

Could they be some of the stolen cartridges? Frank wondered.

Suddenly, Frank heard a sound behind him. He spun around and found himself facing a man in a dark suit. Frank recognized him as the broad-shouldered, ruddy-faced Omega executive that Joe had confronted in back of the hotel the night before.

The Omega executive scowled at Frank and raised an arm in his direction.

In his hand was a pistol. And it was pointed directly at Frank's chest!

9 The Mystery Solved?

"What are you doing here?" said the executive in an accusing voice. "You know that you're trespassing, don't you?"

"There are worse crimes than trespassing," said Frank as he waved his hand at the piles of cartridges stacked on the tables. "Why do you have all these Videomundo games lying around?"

"Oh, that's right," said the executive, the hint of a smile crossing his lips. "You're one of those kids from the hotel last night, playing secret agents in search of the stolen video game cartridges."

"That's me," said Frank. "And we're still searching."

"All of these cartridges were obtained by legitimate means," said the executive. "Some of them were purchased in stores, some of them were imported from Japan, and a few others were obtained from, ah, shall we say, friends of ours at Videomundo."

"Spies?" asked Frank.

"That's not how we think of them," the executive said. "It's common industry practice. Videomundo does the same thing to us. We even know who their 'spies' are among us, but we let them go on working here."

"But if you know who the spies are, why don't you just fire them?" asked Frank.

"Because this way, we can keep our eyes on them. If we know who they are, we won't let them work on top secret projects," the executive answered.

"Well, that still doesn't solve my problem," said Frank. "Somebody's been stealing video game cartridges from the tournament players."

"That's too bad," said the executive, "but it's not the end of the world. Videomundo is a big company. A few stolen cartridges are a drop in the bucket to them. I'm sure the company will replace them."

"Whoever is behind it has also threatened our

lives," said Frank. "They've tried to kill me and my friends."

"That's worse, I agree," said the executive. "But I'm afraid there's nothing that Omega can do about it."

Frank paused and caught his breath. The Omega executive's steely gaze was unwavering, and he was still holding the gun at arm's length. For a moment, Frank wondered what the man was thinking and whether he was actually planning to *use* the gun.

"You can stop pointing that gun at me," suggested Frank.

The executive looked down at the weapon in his hand and laughed. "Gun? What gun?"

He turned and pointed the gun at a video game machine on the far side of the room. Frank cautiously turned around and faced the monitor. What he saw was a shooting gallery game, with revolving targets and mechanical ducks quacking their way across the screen. The executive pulled the trigger, and one of the ducks fell over with a squawk.

Frank's shoulders sagged. "A light gun."

"Right," said the executive, tossing the toy gun onto a table. "I thought I'd give you a scare. Now, get out of here, before I call the police and give you an even bigger scare."

He opened the door of the room and ushered

Frank into the lobby. "I'll see to it that Mr. Gensher sends your friends back out to you—after they've finished their tour, of course. It was a pleasure meeting you."

After the executive pulled the door to the lobby firmly shut, Frank stared drearily at the paneled wall and mumbled, "The pleasure was all mine."

The receptionist gave Frank a curious look, then turned back to her work. Frank settled onto a stylish but uncomfortable sofa and thought about the case. Someone had stolen Joe's bag of cartridges, and then tried to swipe Chet's Hack Attack game—twice. Frank shook his head. A piece of the puzzle was definitely missing, but what was it? Frank looked up, and noticed that Joe and Chet had reappeared.

"What happened?" asked Joe.

"Yeah, where did you go?" Chet added.

"I'll tell you in the elevator," said Frank.

On the way down, Frank told his companions about his confrontation with the Omega executive, reluctantly admitting how he had fallen for the light-gun gag.

"Sounds like he got a good laugh at your expense," said Joe.

"It didn't sound like he was exactly laughing," added Chet.

"Neither was I," Frank said. "I still don't know

about these guys. Everything he told me sounds reasonable, but that doesn't tell us who's stealing those game cartridges back at the hotel."

"Maybe we should do some more snooping," Joe suggested.

"Not in the Omega offices," said Frank. "That guy's ready to call the cops if he sees my face again."

"Think there's a back entrance to this place?" asked Chet.

"It's worth a look," said Frank.

When they reached the ground floor, they exited the building and looked around. Frank noticed an alley halfway down the street and suggested that they look into it. Another alley cut across the first alley, running in back of the building where Omega had its offices. A familiar-looking truck, with the name Omega Corporation on its side, was parked at a small loading dock.

"That was the truck we saw in back of the hotel last night," Joe said.

"Yeah," said Frank, "maybe we should take a look inside."

He mounted the small platform that projected from the rear of the truck. "We're in luck," he announced. "The doors are unlocked!"

Frank lifted the latch that held the doors closed and popped them open. Then he stepped inside, Chet and Joe right behind him.

The inside of the truck was dark, but Frank could make out the silhouette of several boxes. He bent down and examined one.

"These look like that box we saw the Omega guy carrying last night," said Frank.

Chet opened a box and reached inside. "They're full of video game cartridges!" he said, pulling one out and examining it.

"Who made that cartridge?" asked Frank.

"Videomundo," said Chet.

Joe opened another box. "More Videomundo cartridges."

"This looks awfully suspicious," said Frank. "But there's no way to tell if they're stolen."

Suddenly, there was a thumping sound from the front of the truck.

"Whoops!" said Joe. "Somebody's getting into the cab of the truck!"

"Let's get out of here," said Frank. But before he could get to the back doors, the truck lurched forward as the driver gave it gas, and Joe, Frank, and Chet ended up sprawled on their backs.

Joe got back on his feet and leaned on the side of the truck. "Come on, guys," he urged. "We'll have to jump out."

"We can't!" Frank responded as he stood up. "We're moving too fast."

"Oh, no," moaned Chet. "We're trapped!" He rushed to the back of the truck. Through the

89

open back doors, he, Frank, and Joe could see the loading dock slipping rapidly away. "What are we going to do?" asked Chet.

"Wait for the driver to stop," said Joe.

"He'll probably stop when he notices the back doors are still open," said Frank.

"And then he'll find us hiding in the back of the truck," said Chet. "Great!"

The truck swung around a corner into another alley. The three teenagers were thrown violently against the inside walls, but the driver had no way to see into the back of the truck. Joe slid sideways and landed on top of a box of video games.

"Ouch!" said Joe. "Who taught this guy to drive?"

"You'd think he didn't know there are three guys trying to stand up back here," said Frank. "Wouldn't— Whoa!"

With a roar, the truck accelerated, and Frank reeled toward the back doors. Stumbling helplessly, he plunged through the rear entrance and into empty space. He grabbed the inside handle of one of the loosely flapping doors just in time to keep from being knocked to the pavement.

"Help!" Frank shouted, dangling from the swinging door just inches from the back of the truck. "Somebody give me a hand!"

"Here," said Joe, coming back to his feet and reaching out to his brother. "Grab hold of me!"

"Wait!" said Frank. "I might pull you out, too!"

90

The elder Hardy was holding desperately to the door, his feet nearly scraping the street. His heart was racing as he mustered up all of his strength to hold on. He then swung a foot up onto the floor of the truck, and Joe grabbed ahold of it. Frank swung his other foot up and Chet grabbed his leg. Frank was dragged inside, where he collapsed on the floor of the truck. After lying motionless for a moment to catch his breath, Frank gasped, "I think we've had enough excitement for today. What do you say we go back to the hotel and hide under the covers until tomorrow?"

"Very funny," said Joe. "How would we protect our reputations as the best detectives in the western world if we stayed in bed all day?"

"How did we get our reputations as the best detectives in the western world, anyway?" asked Frank with a puzzled look on his face.

"I think it has something to do with our bravery in the face of—"

"Sorry to interrupt, guys," said Chet, "but I think the truck's slowing down."

There was a grinding sound beneath the truck as the brakes engaged, then the truck pulled to a halt. Joe peered out the back door.

"It looks like the driver's stopped at a light," he said. "Let's go!"

Frank, Joe, and Chet jumped out of the back of the truck and hit the ground running. As they headed away between two lines of cars, Joe noticed that the driver of the truck, apparently having heard them bail out, was leaning out the window of the cab. It was the same burly truck driver they had seen with the two Omega executives the night before.

"Hey, you kids!" he shouted. "What are you doing in the back of my truck?"

"Uh-oh," said Frank. "I think our cover's been blown."

The driver opened the door of the cab and began to climb out. "Come back here!" he yelled. "Did you steal something from my truck?"

"He looks angry," said Chet, running between cars. "I don't think we'd better stick around."

"I don't plan to," said Joe. The driver of a brown sedan honked his horn loudly as Joe stepped in front of it. "Keep your cool, mister," Joe yelled. "We're getting out of your way."

"Speed it up," said Frank. "That truck driver's coming after us."

As more drivers began to honk their horns in a noisy chorus, the truck driver started running through the traffic after the three teenagers. But Frank, Joe, and Chet had a comfortable lead over him and managed to lose him in the crowd after only a couple of minutes.

"Maybe snooping in the back of that truck wasn't a very smart idea," Joe said sarcastically.

"It sure didn't give us any clues," said Frank. "For all we know, that Omega guy was telling the truth about getting those cartridges through legitimate channels."

"Why would they want *my* Hack Attack cartridge, anyway?" asked Chet. "They probably have plenty of copies of Hack Attack already."

"Chet's got a point," said Frank. "We have no proof that Omega *didn't* steal the cartridges, but maybe we should look around for some other suspects before we get back to them."

"So what do we do now?" asked Joe.

"I think we should stop at that pizza place," Chet suggested, pointing across the street.

"Good idea," said Frank. "And then we should get back to the hotel."

"And start from square one again," Joe added.

When Joe, Frank, and Chet walked back into the hotel lobby, they found Nick Phillips sitting in a chair with a dejected look on his face. He nodded briefly as he saw his friends enter.

"Hi, Nick," said Joe. "Still thinking about the semifinals?"

Nick shrugged. "I'm just angry that I didn't do better. I *should* have done better."

"What are you talking about?" said Frank. "You made the finals. You should be jumping up and down with excitement."

93

"Yeah, sure," said Nick. He stood up and walked past the others. "Listen, I don't feel like talking about it right now, okay?"

"Whatever you say," Joe said, as Nick strode back to the elevators.

"That guy's got a problem," said Chet.

"Yeah, I really don't understand him," said Joe.

"What's this?" said Frank, bending over and picking up a slip of paper off the sofa, where Nick had been sitting. "Looks like Nick dropped something. Hey, Nick!" Frank waved after him, but it was too late. The elevator doors slammed shut and Nick vanished.

"Too late," said Joe. "You can give it to him later. What did he drop?"

"Looks like a message," said Frank, unfolding the slip of paper. "It says 'SING EVERY NICE SONG WITH EASY NOTES.'"

"What does that mean?" asked Joe.

"Sounds like a song lyric," said Chet.

"Or a secret code of some kind," said Frank.

"Why would Nick be carrying something like that?" asked Joe.

"I don't know," said Frank. "I'll ask him about it next time I see him." He stuffed the slip of paper in his shirt pocket.

Steve Lewis strode into the lobby and paused when he saw the Hardys. "Ah, just the people I was looking for," he announced. "I've got good news for you, Joe."

"Great," said Joe. "I could use some good news."

"We've found your stolen video games," Steve told him.

"Hey, that's great!" Joe said. "Where did you find them? Do you know who stole them?"

"Yes, I do," said Steve. "And I'm afraid that's the bad news."

"I hate these 'good news, bad news' jokes," said Frank.

"Come on into my office," said Steve, waving the Hardys and Chet into the adjoining corridor. They followed him into the tiny room where he worked.

"Here's your video game thief," he said, indicating a familiar figure sitting next to the desk.

Joe's jaw dropped as he turned his head and saw who was under the guard of a heavyset security officer.

Sitting in a chair, his eyes downcast and his head bowed, was none other than Jason Tanaka!

10 Smoke Screen

"Jason!" cried Joe. "What are *you* doing here?"

"I-I'm not sure," stuttered Jason. "They claim I stole the video games, but I didn't."

"There must be a mistake," Frank said to Steve. "Jason wouldn't be behind the thefts. He's just not the kind of guy who would do it."

"Yeah," said Joe. "Besides, we saw the thief. He didn't look a bit like Jason. In fact, Jason was with us when my games were stolen."

"I don't care what you say," said Steve. "I caught Jason with the evidence. My guess is that he hired that other guy to steal the games for him. The police will be questioning him later, so maybe we'll find out more then."

Jason looked up at Joe with a pleading expression in his eyes. "I really am innocent," he said. "I was sitting in my room playing Hack Attack when there was this loud knocking. I opened the door, and these security guards came bursting in, along with Mr. Lewis. They said they wanted to search my room."

"We'd received an anonymous tip that the stolen cartridges would be found there," said Steve. "Sure enough, they were in the closet in his room."

"They opened the closet and pulled the bag full of cartridges out," said Jason, "but I don't know how it got there. It wasn't there this morning."

"I find that hard to believe, Jason," said Steve. "Does anyone else have a key to your room?"

"Well, no," Jason said tentatively.

"Then how could anyone get into your room to plant the cartridges?" Steve asked.

"I . . . I don't know," Jason said.

"The maid has a key to the room," Joe said. "Maybe she did it."

Steve gave Joe a weary look. "You think the *maid* wanted to frame Jason for the crime? What was her motive? Blackmail? Sheer nastiness?"

"Maybe somebody else bribed the maid to do it," Frank suggested.

"You'll have to do better than that," said Steve.

"Unless you can come up with some actual evidence that such a thing happened, I'm afraid Jason is in very hot water."

"Hold it!" said Joe. "All the evidence indicates that the thief was after Chet's Hack Attack cartridge. Why would Jason be after that?"

"That's for Jason to tell us," said Steve. "I've asked him, believe me, but he won't tell me."

"I *can't* tell you," said Jason, "because none of this is true. I didn't hire a thief to take the cartridges. I wasn't trying to get Chet's Hack Attack cartridge. I—I—" Tears began to form in the young man's eyes.

"Easy, Jason," said Joe. "We'll do everything we can to find the real thief. We'll clear your name."

"By the way," asked Frank, "where *is* Chet's Hack Attack cartridge?"

"I've got it right here," said Steve, picking the cartridge up from his desk. "Jason was playing it when we entered his room. I'm going to lock it in the safe to make sure nothing happens to it."

"Oh, no, you don't!" said Chet. "That's my cartridge and nobody's going to take it away from me, not after all I've been through trying to protect it from thieves the last couple of days."

"I don't advise that you keep this on your person, Chet," said Steve. "I can give you a new Hack Attack cartridge, or I can give this one back to you after the tournament, but there's been too much trouble surrounding this cartridge, and I don't want to risk any more. This tournament is my responsibility, after all."

"What are you risking?" said Frank. "If Jason is the cartridge thief—and you seem to be pretty sure that he is—then the cartridge should be perfectly safe, now that you've caught him."

"Right," said Joe. "So give Chet back his cartridge, Steve."

With a sigh, Steve picked up the cartridge and handed it to Chet. "I guess you've got logic on your side. But I still think you ought to take a new cartridge, Chet. I can get you one with no trouble."

"Sorry," said Chet, holding the cartridge to his chest. "I want *this* cartridge."

There was a knock at the door. Two police officers stepped inside and nodded to Steve.

"You called for us?" one of them said.

"Yes," said Steve. "I've found our video game thief. It's this young man here."

"Congratulations," said the officer. "We'll take him off your hands."

Jason stood up, and one of the officers handcuffed him, as Steve explained what had happened. Then the policemen led Jason to the door.

"Joe," Jason said, turning back as he was being escorted from the room, "I forgot to tell you. I found a back door in Chet's cartridge!"

"Come on," said the officer on Jason's right.

"You can talk to your friends later—if you're lucky."

"What was he talking about?" asked Steve, after Jason was gone from the room. "A back door?"

Frank shot Joe a look, which Joe knew meant he shouldn't reveal too much about what they knew of back doors.

"I'm not entirely sure," said Joe. "It has something to do with a conversation we were having the other night."

"There's nothing more we can do here," said Frank. "Let's go."

"I'm sorry about your friend," said Steve, as the Hardys and Chet walked out the doorway. "I wish it hadn't happened this way. But all the evidence points to Jason. I wish it didn't, honest."

"We believe you, Steve," said Joe. "You're just doing your job."

"Something's still fishy, though," said Frank. "I think we'll do a little more looking around."

"Feel free," said Steve. "If you find anything, let me know."

The Hardys and Chet walked down the hallway as Steve closed the door to his office. "Steve sure is anxious to get Chet's cartridge into the safe," said Frank. "Do you suppose he knows something we don't?"

100

"Yeah," said Chet. "You'd think he didn't trust me with it or something."

"Maybe he has a point," said Joe. "Give me that cartridge, Chet. I'm going to keep *my* eyes on it for a while."

"No way," said Chet. "You heard what I told Steve. This cartridge and I have been through a lot together. I'm not letting it out of my hands again."

"Better do what Joe says, Chet," said Frank. "The cartridge thief is still on the loose—we all know that he is—and he thinks that you've got the cartridge. So it'll be a lot safer with Joe."

"Oh, all right," said Chet, handing the cartridge to Joe.

"Now, what do we do about Jason?" Frank asked. "We know he's not guilty, but how do we prove it?"

"By finding the real thief," said Joe.

"Where do we start?" Chet asked.

"The men from Omega?" suggested Joe.

"That sounds like the title of a science fiction movie," said Chet.

"It's too late to go back to the Omega offices," Frank said. "They'd be closed now. And I don't think they'd let us in, anyway. Let's try to come up with some new leads. Who else would have a motive for snatching those cartridges?"

"Maybe someone's out to get Jason," said Joe.

"They could have deliberately framed him for the crimes to get him out of the way."

"Who would want Jason out of the way?" asked Chet.

"Everybody else in the contest," said Frank. "Jason is blowing *them* away."

"Especially Bill Longworth," said Joe.

"Yeah, I wouldn't put it past him to have something to do with this," Frank said.

"Maybe we should pay him a visit," said Joe, with a gleam in his eye.

"Just a polite social call," said Frank. "Let's do it."

A few questions at the front desk told them where Bill Longworth's room was. They walked over to the elevator bank, and Joe pressed the up button. When the elevator arrived, Joe, Frank, and Chet walked inside. During the ride up to the fourteenth floor, Joe was formulating the questions he would ask Bill.

The elevator door opened on fourteen, and Joe led the group to room 1402. He rapped on the door.

"Who is it?" a familiar voice called.

"Your fan club," Joe said. "We just want to talk with you, Bill."

"Go away," Bill said. "I'm playing Hack Attack. I don't want to talk to anybody."

"Open up, Bill!" said Joe, knocking louder. "This is important. We *have* to talk to you!"

102

The door popped open, and an angry Bill Longworth looked out. "You guys!" he snapped. "What do you want, Hardy? Trying to sabotage my game practice so you can get the edge on me tomorrow?"

"We want to talk to you for a few minutes, Bill," said Frank.

"Give me one good reason why I should talk to you," Longworth asked.

"Jason Tanaka is in jail," Joe told him.

Longworth's face fell in astonishment, then he broke into laughter. "Ha! That's terrific! With Tanaka out of the way, I've got a clear shot at the Hack Attack championship!"

"And that's why we want to talk to you," Frank said. "Did you have anything to do with Jason's going to jail?"

"What?" asked Longworth. "I don't even know *why* Jason went to jail. And I don't particularly want to know, either."

"I don't like your attitude," Joe growled at Longworth. "We think somebody framed Jason, and we want to find out why. From where I'm standing, it looks like you had the best motive of all."

"I didn't frame him, Hardy," said Longworth. "But I almost wish I had. It couldn't have happened to a nicer jerk!"

Longworth slammed the door closed in Joe's face. Joe immediately banged on the door with his fist, and said, "Longworth, we're not finished with you. Open up!"

"Come on, Joe," said Frank, pulling his brother out of the doorway. "This isn't doing us any good."

"I don't care!" shouted Joe. "Did you hear what he said about Jason?"

"Yeah, we heard," said Frank. "It's not worth getting angry over. Longworth is one of life's mistakes."

"It's not too late to correct the mistake!" snapped Joe, but the energy was going out of his anger. "Oh, well. I guess it doesn't matter. The worst punishment for guys like Longworth is that they have to go through the rest of their lives being themselves."

"That's the idea," said Frank. "Come on, let's get out of here."

"I'm way ahead of you," said Chet. "The elevators were down this way, weren't they?"

"Yeah, they were over—"

Suddenly, Frank heard a muffled explosion directly in front of where he and his brother were standing. A cloud of thick, foul-smelling smoke rose into the air, engulfing Frank and blinding him. He coughed and gasped for air.

"I can't see!" shouted Frank. "What happened?"

"I'm not sure," said Joe. "I think it's a—"

A loud shout interrupted Joe's comment. It was followed by the sound of a struggle and a thudding noise like a body falling to the floor.

11 Interrupted Tournament

"Who knocked me down?" Frank heard Chet shout from below him in the smoke. "Hey, get your hands off me, Joe!" Chet yelled.

"I'm not touching you," said Joe, between coughs. The smoke was burning his eyes and throat. And it was getting more and more difficult to breathe.

An unexpected voice spoke. "Where's the cartridge, kid? I thought you had it."

"Who is that?" asked Frank, groping blindly in the smoke.

"I recognize that voice," said Joe. "It's the guy

who stole my cartridges—and ransacked our room!"

Joe plunged through the smoke in the direction from which the voice had come. He stumbled against a slender but wiry form. "Gotcha!" Joe called out as he grabbed the thief.

But the culprit wriggled out of Joe's grasp. Suddenly, Joe felt a hand rake across his cheek.

"Oof!" Joe cried out, rubbing his stinging face. "Get your hands off me."

"Out of my way!" barked the man.

"Hey," said Joe, "you want the Hack Attack cartridge?"

"Yeah," said the voice. "Who's got it?"

"I do," Joe said, "and you can't have it."

He swung wildly at the source of the voice and felt his fist connect with someone's flesh. There was a groan and the sound of someone staggering backward.

Joe rubbed his eyes. They burned as if someone had poured chemicals into them, but he also sensed that the smoke was beginning to clear. A moment later he could see the hallway again.

There was no sign of the attacker. Chet was rising from the floor, where he had been knocked down, and was dusting off his clothes.

"What happened?" Frank asked Joe. "I heard you and some guy yelling at each other, then nothing."

"I clipped him on the jaw," said Joe, "but

apparently I didn't hit him hard enough. He got away."

"Are you okay, Chet?" Frank asked.

"Yeah," Chet said. "He knocked me down, but he didn't hurt me. I felt him frisking me, trying to get the cartridge back. I guess it's a good thing I left it with Joe."

"Lucky for you, Chet, but I'm not sure it was smart telling the thief you had the cartridge," Frank said, turning to his brother.

"Sorry," said Joe. "I just blurted it out. Here. You'd better take it now." He pulled the cartridge out of his pocket and handed it to Frank.

"Look at this," said Chet, pointing to an object on the floor. "It looks like a burned-up smoke bomb."

"That's exactly what it is," said Frank. "Somebody set off a smoke bomb to trap us."

"Listen," said Joe. "We now know for sure that Jason didn't have anything to do with the cartridge thefts."

"Right," said Frank. "Jason's in jail, and this guy is still trying to get the cartridge."

"So let's talk to Steve Lewis," Joe suggested.

When they arrived back at Steve's office, however, it was locked; Steve was nowhere around.

Joe looked at his watch. "Well, it may be too late to worry about it, anyway. I've got to get back to the room if I'm going to be in any shape to compete in the Hack Attack finals tomorrow."

"I don't think there's much else we can do tonight," said Frank. "Let's get some rest."

"Rise and shine!" Joe heard Frank call out early the next morning.

"Ugh," Joe answered. "What time is it, anyway?"

"Time for you to get up and eat a breakfast of champions," Chet said. "Today's the day you'll be crowned the new Hack Attack champion!"

"And today's the day we'll be fifty thousand dollars richer," Frank added.

A half hour later, the boys had showered and dressed and were sitting in the hotel coffee shop, eating breakfast.

"I definitely think we should talk with Steve this morning about Jason," Joe said as he lifted a forkful of pancakes dripping with syrup to his mouth.

"After we tell him what happened last night, I'm sure he'll be convinced that Jason's innocent," said Frank, motioning to the waitress for their check.

After the teens had paid their tab, they walked over to the convention center. Just as they were heading to the door, Joe spotted Steve Lewis a few feet ahead of them. He ran over to Steve and told him their story. But Joe was unable to sway Steve's opinion about Jason.

"It doesn't prove anything that this crook is

still running around after Jason's out of the way," he told them. "The thief could be working with Jason. Maybe he hasn't got the word that Jason's in jail. Or maybe Jason's paying him to keep up the thefts so that it'll look like he's innocent."

"You really are a hard case," said Joe. "What will it take to prove that Jason didn't have anything to do with the crimes?"

"Solid evidence," said Steve, "and you don't have any yet. Find me the real culprit, and I'll tell the police to let Jason go. But I'm not holding my breath until that happens."

As the Hardys walked away, Joe muttered, "Sometimes I'd like to hold Steve's breath for him."

"Take it easy, Joe," said Frank. "We'll find the real thief yet. In the meantime, you've got to play the best game of Hack Attack you've ever played in your life."

"Here goes," said Joe, as Frank left to join Chet in the viewing stands. Joe mounted the stage and took a seat at his video game station.

A few minutes later, Steve Lewis stood at the podium and gave the customary speech. Then the video game consoles blinked to life and the games began.

Joe picked up his "passenger" and began the long drive, this time to Kansas City. It was a relatively uneventful trip. On the last leg of the journey a tornado chased Joe's taxi across the plains of the Midwest, threatening to blow him off the road. At one point, the cab was actually blown high into the air, but Joe had picked up a parachute during his previous bonus round and used it to get the cab safely back onto the highway, actually gaining considerable distance in the process. He arrived in Kansas City with his first cab intact. As his passenger left the cab and he collected his fare, his score rose quickly.

His second fare was for Seattle, Washington, and required a dangerous detour around the Mount Saint Helens volcano, which was always threatening to explode during the game. But Joe was already past the volcano when it erupted, and he managed to stay just ahead of the rolling wave of lava until he reached the city.

The third fare took Joe to New Orleans, where the computer played lively jazz music, which Joe listened to over the pair of headphones supplied at his video game station. By the time Joe had picked up his fourth passenger, who was heading for Washington, D.C., Joe knew that he was playing as well as he ever had. From the stage, the players could not see their own scores, but Joe felt a rush of adrenaline that told him he was playing at peak form. Maybe I'm really going to win this tournament, he thought.

And then he remembered Jason. If anyone deserved to win the tournament, it was Jason. But Jason was locked away someplace for a crime that he hadn't committed, and he wouldn't have a chance to win the tournament. The thought made Joe's heart sink.

Abruptly, the image on his video game console winked off.

What is this? Joe wondered. Just when he was tearing up the competition with his best score ever, his machine had stopped working.

As he looked away from his monitor, he realized that it wasn't just his machine that had stopped working—all the contestants were staring at blank screens.

And then the lights went out and the room was plunged into darkness.

12 The Secret of Hack Attack

Of all the times for a power failure, Joe thought bitterly.

He heard a babble of voices around him in the darkness, first from the other contestants and the Videomundo representatives who surrounded the stage, then from the audience in the seating section.

Above the sound of voices, he heard footsteps racing across the stage.

They were coming straight toward him!

Someone ran into him at full speed, knocking him off his chair and onto the stage. A hand plunged inside his shirt and groped around, searching for something.

"Let go of me!" shouted Joe, knocking his attacker aside with all the force he could muster.

"Where's the cartridge?" the attacker asked in a familiar voice. "I thought *you* had it now!"

"Think again!" snapped Joe. "You don't give up, do you?"

Joe grabbed his assailant and pushed him to the floor, pinning him by the shoulders in a wrestling hold. The thief struggled hard to get up, but Joe's superior strength kept him on the floor.

The lights flickered back on. Joe looked down at the person underneath him. Sure enough, it was the cartridge thief.

"Got you at last!" cried Joe triumphantly.

Joe looked up and saw three security guards rush onto the stage. One guard was holding a gun. Another was swinging a pair of handcuffs in his hands. Joe let go of the thief and gestured for the guard to put the handcuffs on him.

The guard looked at the man on the floor and blinked.

"Why, it's Denny the Dip!" he said. "Good to see you, Denny! Long time no see."

"Denny the Dip?" asked Joe.

"Yeah," said the guard. "Denny's been hanging around this part of town for as long as I can remember. When he's not in jail, that is."

"Somehow," said Joe, "I have the feeling Denny isn't doing community service work."

"Nah," said the guard. "He's a small-time crook. Pickpocketing, purse snatching, burglary, Denny's into all that stuff. Aren't you, Denny?"

"I try to keep busy," the thief answered.

"So why are you after Chet's video game cartridge?" Joe asked.

"I've taken up playing video games as a hobby," Denny said. "Keeps me off the streets."

Steve Lewis came bounding up the stairs to the stage. "Congratulations, Joe! It looks like you've caught the person responsible for the thefts."

"Now will you let Jason go?" asked Joe.

"I still have to see about that," said Steve, turning to Denny. "Who hired you to commit these crimes?"

"Some kid," Denny said. "I don't know his name. He's Oriental, probably Japanese."

"What?" blurted Joe. "You're lying! Who told you to say that?"

Steve put his hand on Joe's shoulder. "I'm sorry, Joe. I didn't want it to end up this way any more than you did. I hope you believe that."

"I—I don't know what to believe," sighed Joe.

"Get this guy out of here," said Steve to the security guards. "Call the police and tell them what happened. I'll talk to them later."

"What about the tournament?" asked Joe.

Steve glanced at his watch. "It's too late to start

again. We'll have to postpone the finals until tomorrow. You will be able to make it, won't you?"

"Yeah," said Joe. "But I guess my great score doesn't count, huh?"

"I'm afraid not, Joe. Excuse me, I must make an announcement now," said Steve.

Joe watched Steve walk over to the podium and announce to the audience that the tournament finals would resume the next day. There was a disappointed groan, but Steve promised that everyone would be issued passes on the way out of the arena so that they could reenter the next morning.

Joe joined Chet and Frank on the way out of the convention center. He told them what had happened on stage.

"So this guy implicates Jason, too," Frank said.

"Yeah," said Joe. "But I still don't believe Jason is guilty."

"Maybe whoever framed Jason for the cartridge thefts paid this guy to identify Jason as the culprit," suggested Frank.

"That's what I think," said Joe. "But we're still no closer to finding the real thief."

"Do you think that Bill Longworth has anything to do with this?" asked Chet. "He seemed pretty happy that Jason was in jail."

"I don't think Bill's involved. Sure, he's happy

that Jason's out of the competition, but I don't think he's the one behind this," said Joe.

Frank pulled the cartridge from his pocket. "The solution has to be in this cartridge somewhere. Remember what Jason said about there being a 'back door'?"

"Right," said Joe. "Let's go back to the room and look for it."

Once they were in the hotel room, Joe turned on the television and started to plug the Hack Attack cartridge into the game console, but then he hesitated. "Look at this," he said, holding out the cartridge to Frank.

"Look at what?" said Frank. "All I see is a Hack Attack cartridge—and I've seen plenty of those this week."

"No," said Joe, pointing. "Up here in the corner of the cartridge. I hadn't noticed it before."

Frank took the cartridge from Joe and studied it carefully. In the upper right-hand corner of the cartridge label was a tiny blue dot, so small that he might not have seen it if his brother hadn't pointed it out.

"Is there one of those on your Hack Attack cartridge?" asked Frank.

Chet pulled Joe's cartridge out of a drawer and handed it to him. Joe studied it for a moment, then shook his head.

"Nope," he reported. "It's only on Chet's cartridge."

"Why would somebody want to put a blue dot on this cartridge?" Chet asked.

"To identify it," Frank said. "So it wouldn't get mixed up with other cartridges."

"Which means there's definitely something different about this cartridge," Joe said.

"Plug it into the machine, so we can look for the back door that Jason mentioned," Frank said.

Joe put the cartridge into the machine, then grabbed his game controller and began pushing buttons as soon as the start-up screen appeared. But nothing happened.

"This is harder than it sounds," Joe said. "There must be a million different ways that you could press these buttons. We'll never be able to try them all."

"Hold on a second," said Frank, an odd look coming over his face. "Let me see that game controller."

"Sure," said Joe, handing it to his brother.

Frank studied it for a moment. "Look at this little directional pad on the left side of the controller," he said. "It's got four arrows on it, like the points of a compass."

"Of course," said Joe. "That's how you move the taxicab north, south, east, and west."

"I know," said Frank. "But doesn't that remind

you of something?" When Joe shook his head, Frank pulled a slip of paper from his pocket.

"That's the paper that Nick dropped yesterday, isn't it?" said Joe.

"Uh-huh," agreed Frank. "And look at what it says: 'SING EVERY NICE SONG WITH EASY NOTES.'"

"So what?" said Joe.

"So every word in that sentence begins with either an *n*, an *s*, an *e*, or a *w*. As in north, south, east, and west," said Frank.

A look of comprehension came over Joe's face. "I get it! It's a button sequence, like the ones Jason was using to trigger the back doors in the Battle of the Barbarians cartridge!"

"Exactly!" said Frank.

Joe pressed the reset button on the game console and waited for the start-up screen to reappear. Then he pressed the directional controller arrows in sequence according to Nick's code: S, E, N, S, W, E, N.

The start-up screen faded and was replaced with the opening screen of Hack Attack. The cab waited by the curbside as a passenger walked up to the door and got in.

"Nothing happened," said Joe in a disappointed voice. "The game looks the same as ever."

"Give it a second," said Frank. "Maybe something will happen yet."

The cab pulled away from the curb and started dodging pedestrians and other vehicles as it raced toward its destination.

"Wait," said Frank. "Don't play the game yet. I want to see what happens when you don't touch the controller for a minute."

"I'm *not* touching the controller," said Joe, staring at the screen in astonishment. "The game is playing itself!"

13 The Real
Cartridge Thief

As Joe, Frank, and Chet watched in amazement, the cab raced quickly from destination to destination, racking up the highest score that any of them had ever seen.

"Not only does this thing play itself," said Frank, "it plays really well."

"It plays better than Joe does," said Chet.

"It plays better than *anybody* does," said Joe. "Even Jason."

"Do you suppose all Hack Attack cartridges do this?" asked Frank.

"There's one way to find out," said Joe. He

unplugged Chet's Hack Attack cartridge and placed his own in the game console.

When the start-up screen appeared, he began pressing the buttons in sequence. Nothing happened. He repeated the process two more times, but the cartridge refused to respond.

"Nope," said Joe. "Only Chet's cartridge does it."

"Which means that his cartridge has been specially doctored to play the game itself," said Frank.

"Why would somebody want to do that?" asked Chet. "It must get pretty boring watching Hack Attack play itself."

"It's obvious why somebody would do that," said Joe. "To win the tournament."

"But that's cheating," said Chet.

"Bingo," said Joe.

"Chet?" asked Frank. "Do you remember who you got this cartridge from at the swap meet?"

Chet furrowed his brow in thought. "I must have swapped cartridges with everybody there. I don't remember who I got the Hack Attack cartridge from. I don't remember who I got any of the cartridges from."

"Why would somebody trade away *this* cartridge?" asked Joe. "If someone intended to cheat at the tournament, he would have made sure to hold on to this cartridge."

"It must have been an accident," said Frank.

"Somebody confused the cartridge with an ordinary Hack Attack cartridge and traded it with Chet. Whoever did it must have realized his mistake right away. That's why the thief was already stealing cartridges when we got back into the lobby right after the swap meet."

"But why were *my* cartridges stolen?" asked Joe. "Chet had the rigged cartridge."

"Maybe the person didn't know who had the cartridge at first," said Frank. "He might not have been paying close attention to which cartridges he was trading. Or maybe the cartridge passed through several hands before the swap meet was over. It might have been impossible to determine who had it."

"So he went around stealing *everybody's* cartridges, trying to get it back," said Joe. "That makes sense."

"But that doesn't tell us who the cartridge belonged to," said Chet.

"It's not hard to guess," said Frank, fingering the slip of paper he had taken from his pocket earlier.

"Nick Phillips!" said Joe.

"Right," agreed Frank. "He was the one who dropped the paper on the sofa. He must have needed this phrase to jog his memory, so he wouldn't forget how to trigger the back door."

"And that explains why Nick was so upset after the semifinals," said Joe. "If he'd had the cartridge, he would have come in first, so coming in fourth looked pretty bleak to him. Especially because he was afraid he wouldn't get the cartridge back in time for the finals."

"Yeah," said Frank. "He came here with a foolproof plan for winning the fifty thousand dollars—and he accidentally traded it away at the swap meet! No wonder he was upset!"

"But how could he have gotten the doctored cartridge into the tournament?" asked Joe. "The tournament supplies the cartridges. Contestants aren't allowed to bring their own."

Frank furrowed his brow. "I don't know. Maybe he was going to smuggle it in and switch cartridges at the last minute."

Joe grabbed the cartridge and began heading for the door. "Well, never mind about that. I'm going to tell this story to Steve Lewis!"

"Steve wanted concrete evidence to prove that Jason didn't commit the thefts," Frank said. "Well, now we've got the evidence! He's got to let Jason out!"

Joe yanked open the door and headed for the elevator. Frank followed him, along with Chet.

The group ran to the elevator and rode it down to the lobby. As soon as the doors opened, Joe dashed out and led the way to Steve Lewis's office.

Joe plunged through the door of Steve's office and found Steve sitting behind his desk, poring

124

over a stack of papers. The Videomundo representative looked up and stared at the newcomers when Joe dropped the doctored cartridge on his desk with a triumphant smile.

"We've found the evidence you were looking for," he declared. As quickly as possible, he explained what they had learned.

Steve shook his head in wonder. "That's incredible!" he said. "You're telling me that Nick Phillips was going to cheat by using a special Hack Attack cartridge?"

"That's exactly what we're telling you," Joe said.

"Well, I have to believe you," said Steve. "You've got the evidence right here. I'll have to check out the cartridge, of course, but I'm sure you know what you're talking about. You certainly are a sharp bunch of guys."

"Thanks," said Frank. "We like to think we know a thing or two about detective work."

"So Jason can get out of jail now?" Joe asked.

"It looks that way," said Steve. "I'll take care of the details. You kids can go back to your room. You've done a good job here. Congratulations!"

"All in a day's work!" said Joe, smiling modestly. "What do you say we go play a couple of rounds of Hack Attack in celebration?"

"Hardly my idea of a celebration," said Frank, as they left Steve's office.

"I've got to sharpen my skills for the finals

tomorrow," said Joe. "After all, I'll be playing against the great Jason Tanaka."

They entered the elevator, and Joe pushed the button for the tenth floor. As they walked down the hallway to their room, Chet turned to his companions with a puzzled look.

"Did we forget to close the door to the room?" he asked.

Frank glanced down the hallway. The door to the room was slightly ajar, and light was pouring out.

"No, I'm sure I locked it," he said.

"Uh-oh," said Joe. "This looks awfully familiar."

Joe walked quietly to the door and stood to one side of it, gesturing for Frank to stand on the other side. "If there's somebody in there," he whispered, "let's burst in and surprise him."

He kicked open the door loudly and leapt through, followed by Frank and Chet.

Joe stared at the bed in astonishment. Sitting on it were the two thugs who had kidnapped Chet the day before. The one in the jogging suit raised a gun and pointed it at the teens.

"Hi, kids!" he said. "Always good to see you again. And this is definitely going to be for the last time!"

"Well, hello again," Joe declared. "Somehow I'm not surprised to see you."

The two thugs laughed. "We're just doing our

jobs," the one in the knit shirt said. "Just like any honest American."

"Did Nick Phillips hire you to come here?" asked Joe. "Because if he did, it's too late. We've already discovered his phony Hack Attack cartridge and told Steve Lewis about it. His little cheating scheme is up!"

"I'm sure your friend Nick is shivering in his shoes right now," said the thug in the jogging suit. "We'll worry about what Steve Lewis is going to do later. Right now, we want you to take a little trip with us."

"A trip?" asked Chet. "I think I'd rather go home now, thank you. I think this trip to New York is all I need to last me for a lifetime."

"That's one way of looking at it," said the thug.

"Where are you going to take us?" asked Frank warily.

"Down to the subway," said the thug. "Where you're going to meet with a little 'accident.'"

"Yeah," said the second thug. "A mugging. It's an old New York tradition."

"Like kidnapping tourists?" Joe said.

"Yeah, that, too," said the thug.

"That's a weird tradition," said Chet. "Maybe we could just break a piñata or smoke a peace pipe or something."

"Shut up, kid," said the first thug. "That's enough jokes for now."

Frank started to say something, but the first

127

thug opened the door and waved the teenagers out with his gun. "You guys go first. But don't try any funny stuff. Remember, I've got the gun."

Frank walked just behind the second thug as he led the way to the elevator. At the first thug's urging, Frank pushed the button for the lobby.

What now? Frank thought as they rode the elevator down. I have to come up with a plan to get us out of this one.

When the elevator reached the lobby, the first thug nodded toward the hallway that led to the back entrance.

"That way," he said. "We'll go out the back, so we don't attract too much attention."

Frank recognized the hallway as the one where they had followed the men from Omega two nights earlier. Well, he thought, it looks as if Omega didn't have anything to do with the thefts after all. At the end of the hallway, Frank stepped out onto the loading platform, followed by the others.

"Okay," said the first thug. "We're going to go to the Thirty-fourth Street station. I'll have the gun on me at all times, and I'm not afraid to use it in public. Don't try to get too far ahead of me or lose me in the crowd. I'll be all over you like ants on a french fry."

From the other end of the alley, Frank heard the sound of a truck gunning its engine. Frank noticed that a look of surprise had come over the first thug's face. The thug quickly motioned for them to stand toward the rear of the loading platform.

"Hey, that truck looks familiar," said Joe.

"Yeah," whispered Frank. "It's the truck from Omega. They must be coming back for another load of cartridges."

With a loud squeal, the driver of the truck hit the brakes and skidded to a stop. He looked out the window and waved angrily at Frank, Joe, and Chet.

"Hey, you kids!" he shouted. "You're the ones who broke into my truck yesterday! I want to talk to you!"

The burly truck driver opened the door of the truck and jumped to the ground. He began running toward the loading platform with an angry expression on his face.

"What is this?" said the first thug. "Get out of here, man!" He pulled the gun out of his pocket and fired off a shot over the driver's head. The shot rang loudly in the narrow alleyway, echoing off the sides of the buildings. The truck driver's face turned pale.

"Whoops!" he said. "This is worse than I thought. These guys have guns!"

Joe took advantage of the thug's distraction and hit him soundly with his shoulder. The gun flew out of the thug's hand and landed on the pavement below.

"Hey, you'll pay for that!" the thug exclaimed.

"Let's run for it!" yelled Frank. "Before he can get the gun back!"

Chet opened the back door to the hotel, and the trio raced back into the hallway. They were two-thirds of the way to the lobby before they heard the thugs running behind them again.

"We've got a lead on them," said Joe. "Let's head for Steve Lewis's office. He usually has some security people around there—and they've got guns!"

"No!" said Frank urgently. "Not Steve's office! That's not a good idea!"

Joe ignored him, running through the lobby and into the hallway where Steve's office was located. He burst in the door to find Steve, as usual, on the telephone.

"What in the—?" Steve said, as Joe raced through his door, followed by Frank and Chet. He apologized to his caller and dropped the phone back into the cradle.

"It's those two thugs who kidnapped Chet!" Joe blurted. "They're trying to kill us!"

"You've got to stop them," said Chet. "Call security, quick!"

Steve pulled a gun from his desk and held it up. "I don't need to call security. I've got my own protection."

"Well, that's something," said Joe. "But I'd feel better if—"

130

Behind them, the two thugs burst through the door, the first thug waving his gun in the air.

"You're too late," said Chet. "Steve's got a gun. You better throw yours down—or you'll be in a lot of trouble."

"Oh, I don't think that will be necessary," said Steve, smiling at the newcomers. "How ya doing, fellas?" he said to the thugs. "Good to see you again."

"Good to see you, Steve," said the first thug, closing the door behind him.

"What—?" blurted Joe. "What's happening here?"

"Nothing much," said Steve, pointing the gun at the three of them. "I told you kids you were smart."

He leaned back in his chair. "But this time," he said, "it looks like you were too smart for your own good."

14 Into the Underground

"I knew it!" exclaimed Frank, shaking his head. "I tried to tell you not to go to this office," he said to his brother.

"I don't get it," said Joe. "I thought Steve was on our side."

"Why, I *am* on your side, Joe," said Steve reassuringly. "If Chet had only taken me up on my original offer to keep his cartridge in the hotel safe, then none of this would have happened."

"That's why you kept asking to put the cartridge in the safe," said Frank. "You were the one who wanted the cartridge back all along, weren't you?"

"Quite true," said Steve. "That stupid Nick Phillips traded the cartridge at the swap meet and then came whining to me to get it back for him. Of course, I had to help him. I had no other choice."

"Huh?" said Chet. "Why would you help Nick cheat at your own contest?"

"For the money, of course," said Frank. "You weren't helping Nick Phillips cheat. He was helping *you* cheat."

Steve laughed. "I knew you were smart, Frank. I just didn't know how smart." He leaned back and held the gun casually in front of himself, his elbows propped on the arms of his chair. "Nick Phillips wouldn't have had the foggiest idea of how to create a cartridge like that. He was just the lucky fellow I picked to help me."

The glimmer of understanding appeared in Joe's eyes. "So *you* made the cartridge. You used Videomundo's facilities to create a rigged version of Hack Attack, with a special back door built in."

"With breathtaking speed, the boy detective zeroes in on the truth," said Steve mockingly.

"You were cheating your own company," said Frank. "You were going to keep the fifty thousand dollars for yourself."

"What was Nick going to get for helping you?" asked Joe.

"All the video games he could play," said

133

Steve. "Video game players like Nick have simple needs. They don't want money; they just want what money can buy, in this case games, games, and more games. Well, I've got access to all the video games anybody could ever want to play, and I offered him a lifetime subscription. He took it gladly."

"How could you rip off your own company like that?" Frank asked. "Don't you feel any loyalty to Videomundo?"

"Loyalty?" asked Steve. "What in the world for? They don't pay me enough for all the work I do for them. Meanwhile, their top executives earn hundreds of thousands, even millions, of dollars. The chairman of the company earns nearly ten million a year.

"And look at this lousy office they put me in!" he said, waving his arm around. "No more than a phone booth and a closet put together. The executives have three-bedroom suites upstairs, with walk-in kitchens and fully stocked refrigerators. I've got a lousy single room on the first floor. And my office back at the Videomundo building is hardly any better. Why should I feel loyalty for Videomundo? They certainly don't feel any loyalty toward me."

His face was flushing with anger. He paused for a moment and caught his breath. "With the fifty-thousand-dollar prize money I'm, ah, appro-

134

priating from this contest, I've more than doubled my salary for the year. I plan to do it again next year, too. Next year, I'm going to ask them to up the prize money in the contest to one hundred thousand dollars. It doesn't make up for all the complaints I have about the company, but it's a start."

"When did you hire Denny the Dip to steal people's cartridges?" asked Frank.

"Immediately after Nick came to me, telling me that he'd traded away the cartridge," said Steve. "Nick didn't know who'd gotten the cartridge, so I realized I was going to have to look through everybody's cartridges to find it. One of the security guards had pointed Denny out to me the day before, loitering around a street corner. I approached him, and he agreed to help me. And he came fairly cheap."

"And these two thugs?" asked Joe, pointing at the men near the door.

"We like to think of ourselves as gentlemen of the criminal persuasion," said the thug in the knit shirt.

"Friends of Denny's," said Steve. "Denny doesn't do kidnappings, but he was willing to farm the work out. I do appreciate a well-connected thief. Although I didn't appreciate having to bail them out of jail."

"One thing I don't understand," said Joe.

"Why did you try to kill us in the elevator the other day?"

"I had the possessor of the cartridge narrowed down to only a few people," said Steve, "one of whom was Chet. I figured if you three met with an accident in the elevator, I could check out the cartridges afterward and remove the Hack Attack cartridge if I found it. I botched the job, though. Elevators aren't my area of expertise. I didn't know about the emergency cable."

"We could have told you about that," said the thug in the jogging suit.

"You guys are just full of useful information, aren't you?" said Frank. "Were you the ones who shut off the power during the games?"

"No, I handled the power failure myself," Steve said smugly.

"Why did you have to frame Jason?" Joe asked bitterly. "He wasn't involved in this at all."

"I figured it would be useful to have someone to blame for the thefts," said Steve, "so things wouldn't start to look too suspicious. I didn't count on you kids being so persistent. Planting those cartridges in Jason's room and sending him to jail only made things worse.

"But all's well that ends well," he added, pushing his chair back and standing up. "I've got the cartridge back, and I think our friends here were about to take you boys for a little walk. Let's take that walk together, shall we?"

He gestured toward the door. The first thug opened it and stepped into the hallway.

"We'll go out the front door this time," Steve said. "It's faster." Joe looked down and saw that Steve was holding his gun in his pocket.

They stepped through the doors and onto the front sidewalk, past the rows of taxicabs waiting for passengers. "Cross the street," said Steve.

Traffic was light. Frank, Joe, and Chet looked both ways for cars, stepped off the curb, and began crossing toward the subway entrance.

Suddenly, Frank pulled something out of his pocket and turned toward Steve.

"Oh, I lifted this off your desk while you weren't looking, Steve," said Frank. "I think it may interest you."

"What?" said Steve, staring at the object Frank was holding out to him.

"It's your Hack Attack cartridge," said Frank. "The one you rigged for Nick Phillips."

"Give that to me!" shouted Steve. "If anything happens to that—"

"Sorry, Steve," said Frank. He hurled the cartridge into the air. It came down right in the path of a speeding taxicab.

"Oh, no!" screamed Steve. "Grab it!" he yelled to the thugs. "Don't let anything happen to that cartridge!"

The two thugs lunged for the game, but it was too late. The wheels of the taxicab rolled over the cartridge and crushed it into shattered pieces of plastic. Steve roared as though he were in pain.

"My cartridge!" Steve shouted. "It's ruined!"

"Run for it!" shouted Joe.

"Where?" asked Chet.

"Let's head into Penn Station," said Frank. "We can lose them in there!"

They dashed across the street toward the terminal. Frank led the group down the escalator and into the station.

"Where to next?" asked Joe, looking at the maze of passageways that extended around him.

"I don't know," said Frank. "I guess it doesn't matter. Let's make a right."

Frank led the others down a passageway lined with stores and shops, one after the other: newsstands, restaurants, souvenir stands, camera shops.

"Are you sure we can find our way back out of here?" asked Joe.

"Let's worry about that after we've shaken Steve and his thugs," said Frank. As if to lend emphasis to Frank's statement, the two thugs came rushing into the corridor fifty feet behind them, with an angry Steve bringing up the rear.

"Uh-oh," said Joe. "It looks like they're madder than ever. Let's get a move on."

Frank dashed the rest of the way down the passage, the others right behind him. Glancing back at his pursuers, Frank decided to make a right and raced down a flight of stairs. Joe and Chet were at his heels.

They ran past the ticket booth for the Long Island Railroad and past more stores, fast-food joints, and video arcades.

"Where are we, anyway?" asked Chet. "How many stores are there down here?"

"Lots and lots," said Frank. "This is Penn Station. This stuff goes on forever."

They continued to race down the corridor, then veered right.

"Let's take these stairs," said Joe, pointing to a sign that read SUBWAY.

"Good idea," said Frank. "Here come our three friends now."

They skipped down the stairs, only to come up against a turnstile with a slot in it for subway tokens.

"We don't have any subway tokens," said Joe.

"Jump it!" said Frank.

"That's illegal," said Chet.

"I think it's considered okay in an emergency," said Frank, as he leapt over the turnstile. "And this is definitely an emergency."

The sound of Steve and the thugs pounding down the stairs echoed in the air.

"I think you've got a point," said Joe, as he and Chet vaulted over the turnstile after Frank.

There were a few people milling around on the dark subway platform, some of them reading newspapers.

"Maybe this wasn't such a hot idea," said Joe. "It's a dead end. Where do we go now?"

"The tracks," said Frank. "We can go anywhere in New York from here."

"Are you crazy?" said Chet. "I'm not going on those tracks. They're crawling with rats and who knows what else. Maybe we should wait for a train."

"Great," said Frank. "We can take a nice friendly ride with Steve and his chums, who would like nothing better than to practice their subway mugging techniques on us."

"The tracks it is," said Joe. He leapt off the platform and started running down the tunnel. Frank and Chet leapt off a few seconds later and ran after him. A couple of people on the platform raised their eyebrows curiously but said nothing.

The tunnel was dark and seemed to stretch on forever. "Whatever you do, don't touch the rail," Frank cautioned. "You could get electrocuted."

"Do you think they're still following us?" Chet asked breathlessly as he ran behind Frank.

"I don't hear them," Frank said over his shoulder. "But to be on the safe side, I think we should follow these tracks to the next station and go above ground from there."

140

"We've already gone quite a ways," Joe said. "It can't be much farther."

Finally they came to a halt to catch their breath. "I think we've lost them," Joe said, breathing heavily.

"They were probably scared to run on the tracks," said Chet. "I don't blame them."

"Looking for us?" someone said. The teenagers turned to see Steve and the two thugs standing on the tracks—in the opposite direction from the station they had just left. Steve and the thug in the knit shirt leveled their guns on the trio.

"Steve!" exclaimed Joe in surprise.

"We saw you enter the tunnel and decided to head you off at the pass," said Steve. "We went back up and caught a cab to the next station. And now we've got you cornered. This is another New York tradition. It's called a tourist trap."

"So what do you want with us now?" asked Joe. "Your cartridge has been destroyed. Your scheme to steal the fifty thousand dollars is ruined. Why are you still bugging us?"

"Because you're the ones who ruined my plan," said Steve. "I can't let you get away with that. Besides, I intend to pull off the same thing next year and I can't let you blow the whistle on me. I'll just have to postpone my plans a little."

He raised his gun and pointed it directly at Frank. "Say goodbye to one another, boys!"

141

All at once there was a piercing whistle directly behind Steve. Frank looked down the tunnel, which suddenly filled with light. With a thunderous roar, a train came rushing down the tunnel on the same tracks on which everybody was standing.

"It's a train!" shouted Joe with a note of panic in his voice.

"Yeah!" screamed Frank. "And it's heading straight at us!"

15 Quick Escape

Steve Lewis spun around in terror, leaping out of the path of the train just before it could plow into him. The gun flew out of his hand and disappeared somewhere in the darkness. The two thugs also leapt aside, vanishing on the other side of the train.

Moving as one, Frank, Joe, and Chet jumped against the same wall of the tunnel that Steve Lewis had pinned himself against. Frank held his breath as the train rushed by, just inches away from his nose. He could actually see inside the brightly lit windows as they sped past him. Occasionally a passenger would look up and see him standing next to the wall, and a startled look would begin to appear on the passenger's face, before he or she was carried away into the distance.

His body flattened tightly against the wall, Frank turned his head to look at Joe. "Follow me," he shouted, his voice barely audible above the roar of the train.

"What?" said Joe. "Are you crazy? I'm not moving until this train is gone."

"When this train is gone," shouted Frank, "the thug with the gun will be all over us again. Like ants on a french fry, remember?"

"How could I forget?" replied Joe.

Still flat against the wall, Frank began to edge his way down toward Steve Lewis. The Videomundo representative was standing against the wall with a terrified look on his face, as though he were about to go into shock. When Frank reached Steve's side, he grabbed the man by the shoulder, but Steve hardly seemed to notice.

"Look," Frank said to Joe. "There's a red signal ahead. That means the train's about to stop. And as soon as it does, we're going to jump on."

"What about the thugs?" asked Joe.

"I'm hoping that as soon as we get on, the train will start up again," answered Frank.

"Whatever you say," said Joe. He turned and passed the word to Chet.

As the next to last car slid past, the train ground to a halt. Frank grabbed a chain that was attached to the ends of two cars, hoisted himself up and over the chains and onto the platform between the cars. He unhooked the chains and pulled Steve onto the platform with him. Seconds later Chet and Joe jumped up beside him.

As soon as they were all on the train, Frank rehooked the chains, and the train started to move. The two thugs looked up in astonishment as the Hardys rode past them. They started running after the departing train, but they were quickly left behind.

About thirty seconds later, the train pulled back into the station that the Hardys had been in earlier. Frank and Joe pulled the stunned Steve off the train and onto the platform.

"Let's head for the police station," Frank said.

"Yeah," Joe said. "I'll bet Jason won't mind trading places with Steve."

Dazzling rays of light beamed between the stars. Tremendous explosions flashed in the depths of space. Encased in an airtight space pod, the taxicab soared through the heavens at several times the speed of light.

The alien defenders were out in force, firing their laser beams at the valiant little taxicab. But they were no match for the cab's clever driver. Finally, they relented and allowed the taxi to land on the bright green planet that they were protecting.

Joe's heart leapt. It was the first time he had ever managed to take a passenger all the way to Arcturus. He looked at the score. It was his highest Hack Attack score ever!

He wasn't even bothered when he lost his last cab to an Arcturan slime beast a few moments later. If Joe was ever going to win a video game tournament, this was the score that would do it.

He stood and walked to the seat at the edge of the stage, where he sat down and waited to hear the results. A Videomundo executive named John Aherne took the podium and began making announcements.

"Unfortunately," he said, "we have no fourth-place finisher in today's contest finals. As I mentioned earlier, Nick Phillips was unable to take part in today's games.

"However, the remaining three players have made a remarkable showing, with some of the highest scores I've ever seen in a video game.

"The third-place winner is . . . Bill Longworth!"

Bill gave a little nod and looked sour, but at least he didn't complain out loud. Joe even managed to feel a little sorry for the former Hack Attack champion.

"The second-place winner is . . ."

Joe gripped the edges of his seat tightly. Yes?

he thought. Who was the second-place winner? The pause before the name was announced seemed to go on forever.

". . . Joe Hardy!

"And the grand-prize winner is Jason Tanaka!"

Joe and Jason both stood. Jason stepped to Joe's side and gave him a brisk handshake, then the two friends gave each other a big bear hug while the crowd applauded.

"Well," said Joe, "if I had to lose the contest, I can't think of anybody I'd rather lose it to."

"You didn't lose the contest, Joe," said Jason. "If it hadn't been for you and Frank and Chet, I wouldn't be here to win this contest today. So I have to share this victory with you, too!"

"Does that mean you're going to split the fifty thousand dollars with me?" asked Joe.

"Wellllll . . ." said Jason. Both boys then broke out in big smiles. "Don't forget," Jason said, "the second-place winner gets a ton of Videomundo game cartridges. I expect you to show me what you can do with them."

After the awards were handed out, Joe and Jason posed for photographs and quick interviews with reporters. Finally, they managed to get away and meet Frank and Chet behind the stage.

"Congratulations, Jason!" Frank said. "You, too, Joe. There's nothing wrong with coming in second."

"Sure," said Joe. "What's fifty thousand bucks between friends?"

"Don't worry," said Chet. "I'll be in the contest next year. I'll be happy to split the money with you. Assuming you're willing to teach me how to play the game. And loan me your cartridge. I think the pieces of mine are still lying all over the street."

"I'll teach you how to play on one condition," said Joe.

"What's that?" asked Chet.

"That I get to stay home and watch next year's contest on television," Joe moaned. "I don't want to have anything to do with Hack Attack ever again."

NANCY DREW® MYSTERY STORIES By Carolyn Keene